THE
WOMAN
IN THE

BLUE
CLOAK

Also by Deon Meyer

Dead Before Dying
Dead at Daybreak
Heart of the Hunter
Devil's Peak
Blood Safari
Thirteen Hours
Trackers
Seven Days
Cobra
Icarus
Fever

THE
WOMAN
IN THE
BLUE
CLOAK

DEON MEYER

Translated from Afrikaans
by K.L. Seegers

Atlantic Monthly Press
New York

First published in Afrikaans in 2017 as *Die vrou in die blou mantel*
by Human & Rousseau
First published in Great Britain in 2018 by Hodder & Stoughton
An Hachette UK company

Printed in the United States of America

First Grove Atlantic hardcover edition: May 2019

Library of Congress Cataloging-in-Publication data is available for this title.

ISBN 978-0-8021-4723-3
eISBN 978-0-8021-4724-0

Atlantic Monthly Press
an imprint of Grove Atlantic
154 West 14th Street
New York, NY 10011

Distributed by Publishers Group West

groveatlantic.com

19 20 21 22   10 9 8 7 6 5 4 3 2 1

I

12 October

He was hungry and thirsty, frightened, and weary to the very marrow. Adrenaline alone kept him putting one foot in front of the other. Through the dark of night he pressed on, until the horizon changed colour and the world took shape and reignited hope. Shortly before eight, just before the sun breached the horizon towards Rotterdam, the soft golden morning glow opened up the Schiedam market ahead of him, the crowds, the jostling hubbub, and his heart fluttered faintly, hopefully. Perhaps he could escape here. Just disappear.

He didn't look back. He knew they were at his heels. He kept on walking in the same direction, allowing the clamour to swallow him up. Hawkers trumpeted out their wares, folk chatted, laughed, argued, shouted, and a baby cried inconsolably. Hens cackled in indignation, horses neighed, and from somewhere came the deep lowing of a cow. A gallimaufry of competing scents, the smell of fish and shellfish, crabs and prawns and crayfish, singed duck feathers and animal manure, wet earth and pork on the spit and sausage being smoked and – making his knees buckle momentarily, so strong was his desire – a rich yeasty fragrance as a boy with a big basket of fresh round loaves squeezed past him.

He spotted the dark blue coat hanging from the back of the wagon, instinctively knowing that no one was paying it any heed. With one swift motion he snatched it up, a practised thief. Skill born of experience. He doubled the coat over and held it close to his chest. At the back of a cheese stall he dropped to his knees behind the wooden crates, plucked off his hat and left it on the ground behind him, pulled off the smelly, worn brown coat, and left it there too.

The sun broke over the eastern horizon. He put on the stolen coat, stood up, his knees unsteady at first, making him stumble. He set off, hunched over, only straightening up a while later.

He dodged in a new direction, towards Delft.

Still he resisted looking back, he was too afraid they would see him, the four of them. The four who were chasing him, and hunting him.

2

Ironically, whoever had draped her body over the stone wall would have had a view of Murderer's Peak – one of the rugged heights of the Hottentots Holland Mountains that tower over Somerset West.

She was stretched out on the lookout point right at the top of Sir Lowry's Pass, her head to the north, feet pointing south. She was entirely naked, her body waxen pale. The light of the full moon gave her white skin an unnatural sheen, as if she were some saintly creature.

Her eyes were shut. Her right hand rested on her belly, as if at ease. Her legs were crossed at the ankles. The flickering city lights far below, Gordon's Bay, the Strand and Somerset West and even Khayelitsha made for an enchanting backdrop. At a first, quick look she seemed to be resting, or even posing for a photo or a painting. But if you were to look closely, here in the early morning hours, the scene quickly becomes disturbing: the woman naked in the cold May night, her left arm dangling down the wall, oddly angled, knuckles just grazing the strip of green grass. Peculiar stains in her light short-cropped hair, on her head and between her legs. The constant hum of traffic on the busy N2, the yellow glow of headlights coming and going, reflected off the cliff nearby. She couldn't possibly choose to lie, resting like *that*, here. Something must be badly wrong.

Only fifteen kilometres to the east the leopard trotted down the path, the light of the full moon superfluous to her. She was heading north, back to her familiar hunting ground, the high cliffs and ravines of the rugged mountains, her territory, her place of safety.

She had been here two days already, too close to mankind and vehicles, the sounds and smells that made her nervous and denied her sleep, searching for water and prey after the long, scorching summer drought.

This was the route she had come, two tracks twisting down the slope; she wanted to retrace it, then cross the tar road, past the big dam, where she could already scent the water. And then, into the mountains.

A hum made her halt, faint, but getting louder: she recognised it, the sound of vehicles. She saw the glow of the lights, saw and heard two of them right below her, just there in front of her, come to a stop. Voices. The creak of a gate.

She turned back and melted into the shadows of the *fynbos*.

She could not go home tonight.

Two hours before sunrise, at 5:35, a minibus taxi en route from Mthatha to Cape Town turned into the lookout point. The driver needed to relieve himself. He parked and hastily got out. He didn't notice the body on the wall.

His passengers were a group of thirteen women – seamstresses and dishwashers, domestic workers and cleaners – all of them Xhosa. From the second row of seats, one woman spotted the unnatural shape on the wall. She called out, a cry to heaven. The others woke from slumber, followed her pointing finger. They opened the windows and shouted to the driver. He turned and saw it. In his alarm, he dribbled on his shoe, and cursed. He hurriedly zipped up his fly, leaped back into the minibus and closed the door. He switched on the ignition.

No, said one of the women, call the police.

The driver was reluctant. He knew it would cause hours of delay. His employer would not be happy. And this apparently lifeless white woman had nothing to do with him.

He shook his head, and put the taxi in gear.

The chorus from the back was loud, indignant and unanimous: We're not leaving until you phone the police.

He sighed, turned off the engine, picked up his cell phone and called the police emergency number. It rang and rang. While it rang, he got out again and cautiously approached the body. He stared until he had convinced himself that she really was dead. The policewoman who answered the phone asked him to slow down, speak slowly, in English. He reported what he saw, and answered long, detailed questions about the location.

Eventually he could ring off. He hurried back to his minibus, intending to drive away. But the thirteen Xhosa women scolded him again: 'We can't leave her like this, all on her own!'

The lookout point in Sir Lowry's Pass was almost equidistant from Grabouw and Gordon's Bay, so initially there was some confusion about jurisdiction.

The first police vehicle found a remarkable scene, unique to this southern tip of Africa: thirteen women in the last stretch of dark before daybreak, standing in a semicircle around the body and quietly singing hymns, while the taxi driver stood to one side looking on.

More patrol vehicles carrying inquisitive sergeants and constables from the SAPS offices in Grabouw and Gordon's Bay arrived, and one more from Somerset West. By dawn there was a general trampling of the crime scene and a traffic jam on the N2 – with drivers behaving in their usual sheep-like way on seeing a mass of police cars beside the road.

As a consequence, the Somerset West detectives only got there after eight, and the pathologist, videographers, and forensic team only an hour later.

Just before ten in the morning the pathologist announced that the cause of death was most likely blunt trauma to the back of the skull. But she had been killed somewhere else. And it seemed as though the body had been washed with an excessive amount of bleach. Normal household bleach. He could smell it clearly, and the white patches on the head and pubic hair confirmed it.

There was no sign of her clothes or any possessions.

The ambulance transported her, unidentified and anonymous, to the State Mortuary in Salt River.

It was Tuesday, 16 May.

3

On Wednesday morning, 17 May, just after the morning parade of the Unit for Serious and Violent Crimes of the Hawks – officially known as the Directorate for Priority Crime Investigations – Captain Benny Griessel walked down the long corridor of the second floor. He was headed for the office of his colleague, Vaughn Cupido.

He had news to share. And a favour to beg. But it was going to be a mission. He knew Vaughn. They had been working together for nearly a decade, every day.

He knocked on the doorframe of the open door, and walked in. Cupido watched him enter, and said, 'One of these days you're going to fall right through your own arse.' Griessel was eight kilograms lighter since he had stopped drinking and taken up cycling seriously.

Griessel didn't react, just pulled out a chair and sat down.

'Everybody's getting thinner, it's just me getting fat,' said Cupido. It wasn't entirely true. Only Griessel and Major Mbali Kaleni, head of the unit, had lost weight. But Cupido felt guilty, because Desiree Coetzee, the new woman in his life, cooked delicious food. And Vaughn often ate at hers, partly to protect his interests, partly because he really loved her cooking.

Griessel dropped the bombshell: 'I'm going to ask Alexa to marry me.'

'*Jissis.*'

It was the response Griessel had expected. He ignored it. 'I have to find a ring, Vaughn. I need advice . . .'

'Let me get this straight,' said Cupido. 'You've already burned your fingers with a first marriage.'

Griessel nodded.

'And you're an alcoholic.'

'A hundred and forty-seven days clean.'

'And Alexa is also an alky.'

'Seven hundred and sixty-three days clean.'

'She's a rich woman, and you are a police captain who is, financially speaking, *in jou moer*, with all the fees and whatnot for your boy at film school.'

Griessel nodded again.

'She's this famous singing star, and you're a nobody, who plays bass guitar in a geriatric covers band at the weekend.'

'Not geriatric. Middle-aged . . .'

'And in spite of all this, you're going to ask her hand in marriage, and you're going to tell me it's because you love each other.'

'Yes.'

'You've thought this thing over properly?'

'I have.'

Cupido looked at him. A shiver rippled through his body, a tiny shake of the head. He stood up. 'Cool. Let's go. Where do we buy this ring? Sterns? American Swiss?'

'Muhammed Faizal.'

'Oh, I see. You want to start this marriage proposal the healthy way, by buying stolen goods.' And then: 'Love Lips? Is he still around?' as they left.

'Pawnshop in Goodwood.'

'Didn't he used to be in Maitland?'

Cupido was silent during the drive, following Voortrekker Road through Bellville, then Parow, where Griessel had grown up. Benny looked at the endless string of second-hand car dealerships vying for business like invasive weeds, and he thought, nothing has changed in twenty years. And yet, Parow looked better than a decade ago. It was cleaner, neater, more economically active and alive.

Strange how you imagine a place will go backwards when you aren't there to keep an eye on things.

'What's it like, Benna?' Cupido asked out of the blue.

'What?'

'Married life.'

With that philosophical tone showing he was being serious now, Griessel mustn't make fun of him. 'It's not as if I'm an expert witness, Vaughn. I've been married but once, and I was only sober for the first seven years of that . . .'

'But how was that? The sober years?'

Griessel thought about it, and said, 'It was good. It was . . . Hell, Vaughn, I was married at twenty-four, at that age everything is great, and you see no evil.'

'Scares the shit out of me,' said Cupido. 'Every time Desiree says something that could be construed as a reference to a long-term relationship, or marriage, my guts pull into a knot. *Jissis*, Benna, I've been a bachelor so long now, what will I do? And that *laaitie* of hers . . . How can you be a dad for another man's kid? Because he's looking for it, I can see, he's looking for a dad, or at least a father figure.'

A thoughtful silence. Until Cupido said, 'I know it's none of my business, but why now? If it ain't broken, why would you try to fix your relationship with marriage?'

'Because it will make Alexa happy.'

'And you?'

'If she's happy, I'm happy.'

'So that's love?'

Griessel shrugged.

Muhammed 'Love Lips' Faizal's new pawnshop was on the corner of Alice and Voortrekker in Goodwood. 'Cash-cade' was written in big black lettering on a bright yellow background.

They parked opposite, and got out.

'Too clever for his own good,' said Cupido as they jogged across Voortrekker. 'Your pawnshop regular won't have a clue that it's a pun.'

Second-hand chairs were displayed on the pavement, a cluster of bicycles stood just inside the door. The shop itself was dimly lit, because items of furniture were stacked on top of each other up to the ceiling, every available space crammed with furnishings, household goods, appliances, equipment.

Faizal and an assistant were deep in the shop trying to get a table out from the bottom of a stack. He recognised Griessel. 'Hoezit, Benny,' he said, his fat lips forming a smile. 'I'll be with you now,' and he motioned towards the counter at the western wall.

'Okay,' said Griessel. He and Cupido went towards the counter.

Vaughn paused at an arrangement of old 8mm film projectors and cameras. 'Unbelievable how things change,' he said. 'My dada used to have one of these. Your average cell phone takes better video now. From state of the art to antique in half a lifetime . . .'

They both looked up as the front entrance darkened. A young man stood there holding a big, flat square object. He stopped in his tracks, looking in surprise at the pair of detectives; his eyes searched out Faizal, then looked back at the detectives. There was a nervousness about him, followed by recognition: these men were cops.

Since their days as constables on patrol Griessel and Cupido knew this jittery reaction well – the body language of *in flagrante delicto*. The moment stretched into eternity while no one moved, hunter and prey facing each other, sizing each other up, before the hunt began.

Cupido reacted first. 'Hey!' he shouted and started towards the man.

The man dropped the big, flat square object and it fell at an angle against the door. He spun round and ran out.

'Hey!' Cupido yelled louder and set off after him. Cupido in his charcoal-grey suit ('with just a hint of white pinstripe, retro-classic, pappy. Helluva bargain, I've got this buddy who works at Rex Truform . . .'), Cupido in his post-rebellion phase; his clothes a few months back had been an extremely vivid and informal protest against Major Mbali Kaleni's dress code, but now he was back to his dandy old self.

Griessel ran to the door, saw the young man sprinting against the traffic down Voortrekker Street towards the city. Vaughn Cupido was making a brave effort, considering his few extra kilograms and his fancy funeral suit and sharp-pointed shoes, but the suspect was young and fleet of foot. Benny knew he was even less of a sprinter than his colleague. He watched as Cupido had to leap onto the traffic island to avoid being hit by a car.

Griessel didn't think a moment longer, he grabbed a Silverback mountain bike from the bunch at the door, leaped onto it and pedalled furiously.

Across the Alice Street intersection, a Volkswagen Golf with fat tyres blasted sharply on the hooter. Griessel rode to the left lane. He worked the bicycle gears, which were smooth as silk, while the ends of his jacket (brown, long out of fashion, ten years old) flapped in the wind. At the Goulburn crossroad he passed Vaughn puffing hard. Griessel yelled, 'I'll get him,' and pedalled harder, pleasantly aware of the bike's fluid action, aware of his newfound fitness. Thank God this hadn't happened six months ago. He could see the fugitive disappearing to the left down at Fitzroy Street. He saw Lion's Head in the distance, framed by the buildings on either side of Voortrekker; he'd spent eighteen years growing up in Parow and he couldn't remember seeing Lion's Head so beautifully from this angle before. Strange thoughts flashed through his mind. He hadn't raced a bicycle down Voortrekker since he was a boy. The gap between then and now shocked him; how quickly time had flown. And, he thought, that big flat square object that this young man had brought to the pawnshop, at least it was still there, they would be able to see what he had stolen.

And: it seemed that a suspect had brought stolen goods to Muhammed Faizal. That was going to lead to an awkward discussion . . .

And: he swore, twenty-five years ago he would have caught this youngster, he had been quick, in the old days.

And: *jissis*, but this bike was great, much better than his old black and white Giant, already five years old now.

And: fuck, that meant he had been divorced six years already; where did the time go?

He changed gears again, he was going like the wind. He braked for the Fitzroy turn and realised the suspect was heading for the station. He made the turn at the corner by PopUp Tyres, saw he was fast gaining ground on the young man. But was it fast enough, with Goodwood train station just up ahead?

He pedalled faster. In one of the small front gardens an old grandma was watering her plants. She watched as Griessel sped past, shouted, '*Aitsa!*'

The runner was in Station Street, he turned left again, towards the station, only forty metres ahead.

Griessel turned the corner, eyes watering in the wind, spotted the grey station building with its red roof, newly painted and tidied up. Pedestrians stared at the young man sprinting, then at him, as the suspect darted in at the station entrance. Griessel nearly closed the gap, he had to pull the brakes hard, the rear wheel locked and made a high-pitched moaning noise; he threw the bike down and followed the man up the steps to the platform, spotted him dashing past the nose of the waiting metro train. The train began to pull away, forcing Griessel to wait, gasping for breath among passengers who had disembarked, only to see the suspect scaling the high fence on the other side. Benny's body was far too old for gymnastics like that. And then the young man jogged behind the Grand West Casino buildings, pausing a moment before disappearing to turn back and – Griessel was sure of it – wave politely and sympathetically at him.

4

Griessel wheeled the bicycle into the shop, expecting Cupido to ask right away what had happened, but Vaughn and Love Lips didn't even notice his return. They were engaged in a heated argument.

'You tell me how?' Love Lips said with a desperate note in his voice. He was tall and painfully skinny, with abnormally large hands that he was waving about. And those fleshy lips.

'But why do they come here?' Cupido asked accusingly.

'But how do I keep them away? Don't you know what's written on the wall?'

'People of Cape Town, bring me your stolen goods . . .'

'Very funny. What is written on the wall?'

'I don't care.'

'It says: "Cashcade." That means, a cascade of cash. That's why they bring the stuff here. For the money.'

'You think I can't work out what Cashcade means? Which is, by the way, way too clever for your average pawnshop client.'

Love Lips finally spotted Griessel and his whole skinny body was a plea: 'Benny! Tell this man my books are clean. Tell this man that's why you, a captain in the Hawks, for God's sake, are one of my most loyal clients. Tell him . . .'

'What do you want for this Silverback?' Griessel asked and pointed at the mountain bike.

Faizal looked at Cupido. 'You see? You see? Captain in the Hawks, and he doesn't give me grief about stolen goods, he asks me what I want for the bike. Benny, that's your Silverback Sesta, that is top of the range, disc brakes, shocks front and back; for you, as my loyal customer, twelve thousand.'

'*Bliksem,*' said Griessel.

'Negotiable,' said Love Lips. 'Always negotiable.'

'Where are the papers for that bicycle?' asked Cupido.

'In my office.'

'Mohammed is clean, Vaughn,' said Griessel.

Cupido made a noise in the back of his throat. Sceptical. 'So what is in that parcel that our fugitive from justice left behind?'

Faizal tore the brown paper off the flat square object that the young man had dropped inside the door.

It was a painting, a hundred and fifty by a hundred and fifty centimetres, give or take.

'Holy Moly,' said Faizal.

'It's not *that* bad,' said Cupido.

'No, not the quality, the subject matter,' said Love Lips, crumpling the sheets of brown paper and tossing them aside. Griessel picked up the painting, and flipped it right side up. They stepped back to look. It was a nude study in bright acrylics, a woman lying across a bed on her belly; her raised feet – in high heels – were closest to the viewer, her head of wavy black hair was furthest away, the face somewhat veiled and turned aside. Even to their untrained eyes the quality was somewhat amateurish: the scale and perspective were a bit off, but you couldn't quite put your finger on exactly where the fault lay.

'That's unacceptable to you?' asked Cupido. 'That? Bum of a white woman?'

'No, there's nothing wrong with that bottom,' said Faizal, explaining patiently. 'It's the blue.'

The quilt that the woman was lying on was a deep blue. The fabric was draped over the foot of the bed, making decorative folds to shield her bosom, and it dominated the colours of the painting.

'What's wrong with the blue?' Griessel asked.

Faizal sighed. 'Come and look here,' he said and walked further into the shop. He called loudly to the back, 'Harry, put the lights on for us,' and he went and stood between a stack of old government desks and a pile of foam rubber mattresses, where twenty or more paintings were stacked on edge, all more or less square, most large, a few smaller.

The fluorescent lights on the ceiling flickered and lit up.

'Why do you keep the place so gloomy?' asked Cupido.

'Second-hand goods under a spotlight? Clearly you're no retail expert, my bru,' said Faizal, though with only a thin veneer of brotherhood in his tone.

He waited for Cupido to respond. He got nothing. So he turned back to the paintings. 'Look here, the first ten or so,' and Love Lips tilted the paintings slowly, one by one, like the pages of a book. Each painting was of a woman, older women, younger ones, black, white, thin or plump, dressed, undressed. There were only two elements that they all had in common – a woman, and the colour blue that practically always dominated the scene. There was a Xhosa woman with a bundle of firewood on her head, her dress and matching headscarf a deep indigo. A grey-haired woman posing on a chair that looked almost like a throne, the upholstery cobalt blue. A coloured woman shelling pome-granates at a kitchen table. The tablecloth was a blue bordering on turquoise. A white teenage girl leaning her head on a horse's neck. Her riding jacket was navy blue.

'These last few months,' said Faizal. 'They come in here and tune me, "Lips, here's the woman in blue."'

'The woman in blue?' asked Cupido.

'Just like that. The woman in blue. Every time I ask, "What do you mean, 'the woman in blue?'" and then they just tune me, "The grapevine says there's big money in the woman in blue." And I say, every time, "I don't know what you're talking about." Then they tune me, "No, that's the rumour, someone is looking for a classic, original painting, not a print, the woman in blue." As if that's the freakin' title, you understand?'

'The woman in blue.' Cupido tasted the words again as he paged through the paintings.

'Exactly,' said Love Lips Faizal.

'And then, what do you do?'

'I pawn each one as they come in. Everything by the book, though. ID, proof of address, the works. All in the files.'

'How much do you pawn these paintings for?'

'Fifty bucks, mostly.'

'Geez.'

Faizal shrugged. 'That's what the stuff is worth.'

'Mohammed, the engagement rings . . .' said Benny Griessel, because he had already explained to Faizal over the phone what he wanted.

Faizal was grateful for the change of subject. '*Ja*, Benny, congrats, by the way. Alexa is a fine woman.'

'How do you know Alexa?' asked Vaughn Cupido.

'I read the magazines, my bru.' Alexa Barnard had been a famous singer in the eighties, before her late husband and the bottle ruined her career. But in the past few years she had been in the news now and again, focusing on her careful return to the stage, and the record company that she successfully managed now. 'And Benny told me, when he last came to buy furniture here, when they moved in together. We go back a long way, this captain and I.'

Cupido just nodded.

Faizal pointed his thumb at the back. 'The rings are there in the office safe. Come with me.' And as they walked towards the office: 'You know what they say, Benny, the three rings of a relationship?'

'No.'

'The first ring, it's the engagement ring. Then comes the second ring, that's the wedding ring. And eventually there's the third ring. That's the suffering . . .' And Love Lips laughed.

'Inappropriate, brother,' said Vaughn Cupido in disapproval. 'You don't say that to a man who's about to get married.'

'Then I hope it's appropriate to talk about the four "c"s,' said Faizal with a hint of sarcasm and a sidelong glance at Cupido. They sat around the desk in his office, a room that, in contrast to the chaos of the shop, was surprisingly tidy; budget steel shelving along the walls held hundreds of files, Love Lips's proud record-keeping of each and every transaction.

On the desk lay four jeweller's trays lined with velvet, the diamond rings displayed in neat sparkling rows.

Cupido didn't react to the sarcasm.

'Benny,' said Faizal, 'when it comes to choosing a diamond ring, you need to take into consideration . . .' And he raised his big hands and counted off his fingers: 'Cut, carats, colour, and clarity. The better those four "c"s the better the diamond. And the more it costs. You get your very big carats, like this one, very impressive, but the colour and clarity are very iffy, so that's why it's in the below seven thousand tray. This tray here is seven to fifteen, this one is sixteen to twenty-five, and this one twenty-five thousand and above. And to be honest, for a woman like Alexa Barnard we don't really want to look at anything under twenty-five.'

'Ay-yay-yay,' said Benny Griessel despondently.

'Twenty-two thousand rand,' said Griessel as they drove back to the Hawks headquarters in A.J. West Street in Bellville.

27

'I feel you, Benna,' said Cupido. 'But I still think Alexa would be happy with a smaller ring. Or a flawed stone. She's a class act.'

'That's not the problem, Vaughn. Alexa will say we don't even need a ring. But let me tell you when the ring counts. That moment when the friends see it. When they come rushing up saying, "Oh, wow, Alexa, we hear you're engaged, let's see, let's see." You wanted to know what love was earlier. *This* is love. To not let the woman in your life feel ashamed at that moment when she has to show everyone the ring.'

'I see,' said Cupido. And a while later: 'So, basically you're in your glory.'

'Right. I have absolutely no idea where I'm going to find twenty-two thousand rand.'

5

It was like when the dog caught the bus, Sergeant Tando Duba, SAPS detective from Somerset West, would later explain to his colleagues. You're on the lookout for a big fat murder case, because that means attention from higher up, and attention from higher up plus a good investigation plus a conviction meant promotion. And promotion meant a better salary, and, Lord knows, members of the SAPS could always do with a better salary. So, that was the bus all detectives chased: a big fat murder investigation.

Until you were the one who landed the case of the murdered woman lying on the little wall up there on the pass.

The one the newspapers had christened the '*Gebleikte Lyk*' in Afrikaans because it rhymed, and the 'Bleached Body' in the English-language papers because of the alliteration.

Undoubtedly, without question, no two ways about it, a big fat murder case. You got to see your name in the dailies on Wednesday morning, and it was a good feeling, because that was a first for you, the blanket publicity. And your station commander gave you all the help you needed, because the media spotlight was focused on the SAPS office in Somerset West. And the head of investigations in the Western Cape – a general! – phoned you in person to wish you good luck and promise support. And you realised this was a big bus, a fat bus, a dream bus. A bus that could take you a long way.

But then Wednesday passed, and Wednesday night and you make no progress at all. Nothing. After the torrent of breathless publicity you wait for the phone to ring, for someone to come forward with a name, an address and a history of the Bleached Body, so that you can determine a motive, and identify suspects. But nothing. You request the description of every missing person from Cape Town to Knysna, send out bulletins, you and your colleagues phone around and follow up on every angle, but there's nothing to be found. '*Akhukho nto eyichazayo,*' Sergeant Tando Duba told his wife on the phone in their Xhosa mother tongue. Nothing.

And every five minutes the liaison officer comes to ask for news, because the media want to know. Every five minutes, until the media become an angry, hungry beast that wants to devour everything in its path, and you have nothing more to feed it, and know you'll be the next item on the menu if you don't find something.

So you begin to feel just like the dog that caught the bus. Uneasy. Because this big fat bus doesn't seem to be headed for Promotion. There are a whole lot of other possible destinations.

On Thursday morning Tando asked the media liaison officer to leave him alone. After which his station commander called him in and, in his usual wise and easy manner, said, 'Tando, you can see the media as your enemy, or you can see the media as your friend. My advice is: go to the mortuary at Salt River and ask them to make up the face of the Bleached Body, and then get some pictures taken. Publish those photos in the very same newspapers and websites that are bothering you so much. Then let the media work for you.'

Suddenly it felt as if the bus was back on track.

'An engagement ring?' the woman at the bank queried Griessel.

'Yes,' he said.

His loan application lay on the desk between them.

'And this would be for you?' Her friendly intonation seemed to invite him to deny it. He couldn't blame her. Here he was, forty-seven years old, the traces of alcoholism and decades of police work etched into his face, his hair – too messy, too grey – long overdue for a cut. And his eyes, those peculiar eyes that had been described as 'Slavic' – though he had no idea what that meant – showing the world that he had experienced much, seen much, and most of it hadn't been good.

'Yes, it is for me,' he said, deliberately, patiently. At the bank, patience was always the best policy.

'You already have the student loan . . .' As if he didn't know it, all too well. His son, Fritz, was a first year student at the film school, AFDA. It was bankrupting him; their student fees bordered on daylight robbery.

'That's correct,' he said, but felt his heart sinking.

'An engagement ring . . . That's not good security for a loan . . .' She let her words hang in the air, allowing him to come to his own despairing conclusions.

'I can see that.'

'And the establishment where you wish to purchase it . . . That is not one of our approved retailers . . .'

Establishment. He wondered what Mohammed 'Love Lips' Faizal would say if he could hear his Cashcade pawnshop described as an 'establishment'. He'd probably throw those big hands up in the air, and roar with laughter.

'You must decide,' he said. 'But that is where I am going to buy it.' He had done his homework. At the traditional dealers he would pay far more for a ring of similar quality.

He stood up. They wanted him to be more solvent, or provide something to serve as security. They wanted something he could not give them.

She seemed on the verge of asking something, but in the end she just nodded and said, 'I will let you know as soon as possible.'

On the way to his car he wondered why they always went into so much detail about the reasons why you *didn't* qualify for a loan. Why not focus on all the reasons he *could* be trusted with a loan?

He and Alexa discussed everything. Especially since his psychiatrist had told him his drinking problem was rooted in the fact that he didn't talk to his loved ones enough, especially about the dark aspects of his work. But this was one thing that he could not discuss with her. She would immediately want to give him the money to pay for it. And moreover she would not understand his dilemma. Her financial affairs were different, and always had been.

The bank was his only solution. But how did this work now? You banked with the same bank for nearly thirty years, always paying back every last cent you owed them, perhaps a little overdue sometimes, and always with a great deal of effort, but over the years you paid them back every single cent. With interest. Mortgage bond, car payments, personal loans, Karla's student loan, overdraft facilities. Every cent.

But now they have to have a think about it. Because he didn't have a single thing they wanted to take from him.

By five that afternoon Sergeant Tando Duba had sent the digital photos of the Bleached Body's face to the SAPS liaison officer. They decided to forward only one to the press – the one that would give least offence; after all it was the image of a person who had died only days ago.

The liaison officer immediately sent it to all the media on his list.

The *Sun* was the first newspaper to get it on its Twitter feed. The other news publications and websites were hot on its heels. By six o'clock it was the main item on Network24, News24 and IOL.

By eight the photo had gone viral, causing a macabre sensation on Twitter, especially in the age group from fourteen to eighteen.

At half past eight that night Sergeant Tando went home because he'd had no response. No one had the faintest idea who the Bleached Body had been.

The destination of this bus looked increasingly ominous.

*　　*　　*

Vinnie Adonis was one of two men who worked as day shift concierges at the prestigious Cape Grace Hotel on the Cape Town Waterfront.

It was he who tipped the first domino in the management of the Bleached Body homicide. He was fifty-eight years old, but still walked every day from Cape Town Station to work. Just past seven on Friday morning, 19 May, on the corner of Riebeeck and Adderley, he spotted the front page of *Die Burger* newspaper stacked in a heap on the pavement beside the vendor. He registered the colour photo of the strange face, skin bluish-white, eyes closed, with the caption above it: *Do you know her?*

'Yes.' The word formed in his mind, but he rationalised, no, he didn't know her. His mind continued to insist, 'yes,' and he turned and retraced his steps to the pile of papers and had a better look.

'Piracy viewing's a crime, uncle,' said the newspaper seller.

Vinnie chuckled and dipped his hand in his pocket. 'How much?'

'Special price for you today, uncle, eleven rand.'

He dropped three five-rand coins into the boy's cupped hand. 'Keep the change,' and he picked up his newspaper and stared at the photo while he walked.

It's the American woman, he thought. Mrs Lewis. Mrs Alicia Lewis. Not an oil painting, but very pleasant. You got those Yanks who tried too hard to be agreeable to the natives, you got your Yanks who were condescending, and then you got your Yanks who were just normal with everyone. She was one of those. She'd asked him for a couple of things, on Sunday. He thought it was Sunday that she'd arrived.

Yes, he did think the pale woman on the front page of *Die Burger* was Mrs Alicia Lewis.

But was it really?

Vinnie Adonis showed the newspaper to his day shift colleague. 'Doesn't this look like Mrs Alicia Lewis in 202?'

'It does, hey . . .'

'When did you last see her?'

'Now that you mention it . . .'

They weren't sure. They took the newspaper to the assistant manager, who listened to their story, thought about it, and then accompanied them to the manager. The manager sent for the head of hotel security, who fetched the copy of Mrs Alicia Lewis's passport from the file, and all five staff compared the blue-white face of the Bleached Body on the newspaper page with the passport photo. Two of them couldn't see a likeness, two suspected it might be the same person. Vinnie was convinced.

The hotel security manager said he would retrieve video footage from the hotel CCTV cameras, because passport photos could be misleading. The manager said he would knock on the door of room 202 in the meantime.

It was only at nine o'clock that the second domino fell, when the day manager of the Cape Grace Hotel called the number at the end of the article in the paper, and informed Sergeant Tando Duba they had reason to suspect that the Bleached Body was Mrs Alicia Lewis, an American citizen apparently living in London; the address they had on record was 10 Carol Street in Camden Town, London.

'What makes you think it's her?' Sergeant Tando asked.

'Because we've checked the CCTV footage, which by the way is hi-def 720p HD, and the similarities between the photo in the paper and the woman on video are remarkable. Also, according to the video footage, the last time she left the hotel was on Monday morning at nine thirteen. And according to our cleaning team, her room has not been touched since Monday.'

'Oh, shit,' said Sergeant Tando Duba quietly.

The third domino toppled when the station commander of the SAPS in Somerset West called the chief of investigations – the general! – in the Western Cape to inform him that the Bleached Body was most likely a foreign tourist; and what's more, an American-living-in-England foreign tourist.

The general had been in the front line for a long time. He had come up through the ranks, his ability to predict the future had been honed by a wealth of experience, and what he could see here, very clearly, was trouble. He told

Deon Meyer

the station commander of Somerset West that he was genuinely sorry for Sergeant Tando, but in the best interests of all, including the young detective, it would be better to hand this hot potato over to the Hawks.

The station commander breathed an audible sigh of relief. This bus had just gone international, and it was better that he and his people got off. Because there was only one destination for a big fat bus with a foreign tourist as the victim of murder. This bus was en route to the circus.

6

12 October

He stole a piece of salted fish, and then a string of sausage hanging beside the head and trotters of a huge pig. He ate the sausage raw, as he walked. His stomach rumbled and complained, but he knew he needed this fuel, any fuel, urgently.

He avoided the eyes of the market-goers, kept his head down, walked out of the market, north on the Delft road.

Only once he had been walking for fifteen minutes did he look back.

He couldn't see them.

He ate the salt fish beside the Oude Lee, so that he could quench his thirst with water. He didn't linger, drinking long and deep before taking to the road again.

An hour after the Schiedam market, nearly halfway to Delft, he looked back again. There was less traffic and the road was straight. And there they were, the four of them. All dressed in black. Still far off, barely more than specks. But they had been chasing him long enough for him to recognise their shapes. Their purpose.

He groaned in despair. The dark coat, abandoning his hat, it hadn't helped at all.

He couldn't go on much longer. He thought of leaving the road, trying to hide somewhere, but the terrain was too flat around here, and they had seen him now, they had a clear view of him; if he tried to escape across the fields they would know.

They were going to get him.

He lengthened his stride.

7

Captains Benny Griessel and Vaughn Cupido were the two Hawks who caught the bus to the circus. They were high in the Hottentots Holland Mountains, standing at the viewpoint with Sergeant Tando Duba, while the northwester teased Griessel's hair and Cupido's jacket, and the cold front swung its scythe of cloud across the peninsula like a portent.

'Why?' Cupido asked the head of the Unit for Serious and Violent Crimes, Major Mbali Kaleni. 'Why do we always get the case after some rookie has f—' He checked himself – the major didn't tolerate bad language. 'Has messed it up?'

Major Mbali knew Cupido was fishing for a compliment along the lines of how they were such excellent detectives that they could handle anything. She knew her men. Cupido flourished on a diet of positive feedback and praise. But that treatment made Benny Griessel uneasy. Benny didn't like himself much. All he asked for was space and quiet trust and maybe a private word of thanks when a case was wrapped up.

'We don't know that it *is* messed up, Captain,' she said.

'It's always messed up. These station detectives are under-brained, under-trained, over-promoted and over-confident. Generally useless.'

'*Hhayi!*' the major said in Zulu, but in such a way that anyone would know she meant 'enough' and 'basta' and 'stop it' and 'just get out of here.' All that wrapped up in one firm word.

So, they drove off to Sir Lowry's Pass as it was there that the major had arranged for them to start taking over the case. And now here they were in the teeth of a biting wind, with Sergeant Tando Duba showing them photos on his mobile phone, a big Samsung Galaxy Note: images of the Bleached Body draped over the low wall. Duba was a bit intimidated by these two legends. Every detective in the Western Cape knew about Benny Griessel and Vaughn Cupido, the sweet and the sour.

'They say it'll take weeks to process all the forensic stuff they found here,' said Duba, pointing at the area around the viewpoint.

'I don't think they'll find anything,' said Benny Griessel.

Cupido nodded. 'If you're smart enough to wash a body in bleach, you don't leave evidence where you stash it.'

'Okay,' said Duba, ready to learn from the masters.

'You know what bleach does?' Cupido asked.

Duba knew. He had also expanded his knowledge talking to the forensic team. He wanted to say that, but Cupido didn't give him the chance: 'Your household bleach destroys DNA evidence, actually it spoils a lot of chemical evidence. And it masks blood.'

'Not all bleaches,' said Duba. 'Chlorine bleach can make it difficult to see blood, but luminol will still pick it up.'

'Look,' said Cupido, 'there's only one question you want to ask about this place: why did he leave the body here? Why didn't he bury her somewhere? Or just dump it in a more secluded place? That's your first question.'

'Okay.'

'And you also might want to ask yourself how he got the body out of the vehicle, and onto the wall, without being seen from the N2 there,' said Cupido.

'Sometimes there are no cars, for a few minutes . . .'

'Still, it's risky,' said Griessel.

'Have you ever carried a dead body?' asked Cupido.

'No.' The ambulance personnel normally did that.

'Heavier than you think,' said Cupido. 'So maybe, this was more than one guy. And you also start thinking about the vehicle itself. Your ordinary sedan could be a problem. Too low to hide you from the traffic there. Car standing here, open boot, guy taking out something that looks like a body . . .'

'I see . . .' said Duba.

'So, you have to think about a big four-by-four. Maybe a panel van, or a minibus,' said Cupido. 'And you get people to start checking all the N2 traffic camera shots of big SUVs or minibuses that night, with two or more people in them, on the road after dark.'

'I didn't have enough people,' said Duba.

'He's not criticising your investigation,' said Griessel, knowing how people sometimes misread Cupido.

'I'm just putting stuff out there,' said Cupido.

'We did start looking at the traffic. But there were more than six and a half thousand vehicles on this stretch of road that night, between sunset and sunrise,' said Duba. 'And the traffic cameras belong to the province, and tracing all those plates, it's going to take weeks. Months even . . .'

Cupido looked with closer focus at the young Xhosa detective. He knew how complicated the relationship between the DA-controlled province and the SAPS was.

Not always easy to get whole-hearted cooperation. 'Good job,' he said.

Benny Griessel could see that Sergeant Tando Duba was unsure about Cupido's tone. 'He means it,' he said.

'Oh. Thank you.'

'You know those phones catch fire?' Cupido pointed at Duba's Samsung Galaxy Note.

'No, only the new ones, the seven. This is a six.'

'Okay, so he's not useless. Even his docket is organised,' said Cupido as they drove back to the city via the N2. He paged through the dossier Duba had handed over while Griessel drove.

Vaughn studied the pathologist's report in Section B of the file. He read aloud: 'Female, early to mid-forties, no signs of sexual assault, no defensive wounds ... Body comprehensively washed in household bleach ... No fingernail scrapings, no gunshot residue ... Blunt force trauma to the head, shattered the occipital bone ...' Because only he could see the sketch, and he knew the detectives didn't always know the names and precise locations of all the anatomical parts, he touched the back of his head just above the neck, and said, 'It's this one, at the back ... Cause of death is severe trauma to the cerebellum, probably instantaneous. Wound was caused by a single blow of substantial force. Wound comprehensively washed with household bleach. No wound residue, no splinters, no micro-particles. Blunt force weapon probably rounded metal cylinder, approximating five-centimetre-diameter pipe.'

Cupido looked at Griessel. 'One single blow, Benna. Substantial force.'

'Big, strong guy.'

'And not rage, not panic, not overkill. Just efficiency.' They both knew this sort of single wound was commonly found in accidental deaths at home or in traffic. In cases of murder it was common to find more than one wound – signs of struggle, a killer who, either out of rage or panic or desperation, inflicted multiple blows, stab or bullet wounds.

One single, brutal blow from a metal pipe didn't fit a possible opportunistic crime against a foreign tourist who had only been in the country one day before she died.

'Time of death?' Griessel asked.

Cupido scanned the report. 'Probably Monday afternoon.'

Griessel sighed. That meant the crime was already ninety-six hours old. The conventional wisdom was that the first seventy-two hours were critical to an investigation. They were already behind the curve and the gap would probably grow.

In the day manager's office of the Cape Grace Hotel, the detectives compared the CCTV screenshots and the photo of the Bleached Body. They could see similarities, but weren't entirely convinced.

'That's her,' said the concierge Vinnie Adonis. 'Mrs Alicia Lewis.'

'What makes you so sure, uncle?' Cupido asked, always courteous when talking to a coloured man with a respectable, legal, white-collar job.

'I assisted her on Sunday, at my desk, and I helped her again on Monday morning. I'm the person who had the most contact with her.'

'Uncle, are you prepared to go and identify her at the morgue?' Cupido asked.

'If it must be done, I'll do it.'

'Thank you, uncle. Now, we want you to tell us all about Mrs Lewis. Everything you can remember.'

'Okay. She arrived at the hotel on Sunday afternoon, from London. This Sunday, the 14th. I know that, because when she came to ask me some things just before five o'clock, she commented that the weather was so good here, the day before in London it had rained so much. I said, Mrs Lewis, you don't sound like an English lady, and she laughed, and said, no, actually she's from America, but she's been living in London for quite a while.'

'So, uncle, what did she want to ask you?'

'She asked me the best way to get to Villiersdorp. It was a bit funny, the way she said the name, I didn't understand it, "Vil-yees-door" in that American accent. I had to get her to write it down, and then I said, "Oh, okay, Villiersdorp," and she said, yes, she had to go there on Monday, and should she Uber or hire a taxi or a private car, what was the safest?'

'She had to?' Griessel asked.

'Sir?'

'Did she say she *had* to go to Villiersdorp?'

Adonis hesitated and frowned and then said, 'That's a good question, maybe she said she wanted to go, I can't remember exactly.'

'What did she want to do in Villiersdorp?' asked Cupido. 'Did she say?'

'No.'

'Okay, uncle, and then?'

'Then I said, no, everything is equally safe. A taxi or an Uber all the way to Villiersdorp could be very expensive, but she wouldn't have to worry about getting lost. She laughed and said Google Maps was her navigator. She was really very nice; not all the Yanks are nice, but she was. And she said she was going to be here for two weeks, she thought it best to hire a little car, and could I help her. I said no problem, what sort of car did she want, and did she want the car delivered at extra cost, or would she take a taxi to Avis at the airport? She said, no, get them to deliver a medium-sized car, around nine o'clock. I said, right, I'll arrange it. So, Monday morning, she came back to my desk, just before nine, and she and I and the Avis man did the paperwork. And then, at nine thirteen, according to the CCTV, she left with the Avis car keys, a Group E Avis car, silver Toyota Corolla with an automatic gearbox. Most boring car in the country, but what can you do?'

Griessel was going to ask Avis to get the car registration number as fast as possible, but the door opened and the day manager put his head in and said, 'We might have something for you . . .'

They looked at him with anticipation.

'It's difficult to talk to all the staff at once, because they're tied up with work, so we're having small meetings during breaks. And a waitress who works in the Signal just told us Mrs Lewis had breakfast with a man on Monday morning.'

'The Signal?'

'Our restaurant.'

'We'd like to talk to her,' said Cupido.

'Of course. She's waiting for you.'

'Is there CCTV footage of the man?' asked Griessel.

'We'll start looking right away,' said the manager.

'Thank you very much,' said Griessel.

'You're welcome. Look, I . . . I'm sure you're aware of this, but we have Mrs Lewis's home number available. Her London home, I mean. It's on her booking info.'

'We can't call until we've identified the body,' said Cupido.

'Of course, of course.'

8

Cupido drove Vinnie Adonis to the Government Mortuary in Salt River, so it was only Griessel who accompanied the manager to the CCTV monitor room.

The waitress was waiting for them, a young Xhosa woman. 'I thought he must be her grandpa,' she said while they waited to view the right footage on the screen.

'The man she had breakfast with?'

'*Ewe*. He was old, and he was like this.' She held her hand low and curved, to demonstrate the man was short and bent.

The head of security played the video footage of the front lobby back to them at twice the normal speed, until the waitress said, 'That's him.' It took a while to freeze the best image on the screen.

'You see,' said the waitress. '*Utatamkhulu*. A little grandpa.'

Griessel nodded. The man in the image was on the wrong side of seventy, small of stature, back bowed, with a gait that told of old stiffened joints, but there was a lively undaunted, self-assured air about him. His hair was still thick, short and neat, greyed to white and combed back meticulously. His nose was prominent. In his right hand he carried a brown briefcase of soft leather, in his left a grey fedora. He was smartly dressed in jacket, white shirt and tie.

'You're absolutely sure he had breakfast with Mrs Lewis?' asked Griessel.

'*Ewe*. Very sure. She had a cheese and mushroom ome-lette, he had a health breakfast. Muesli and fruit and yoghurt. She was nice. He was . . . white.'

Griessel asked the head of security what time the old man had arrived at the hotel.

'Seven fifteen.'

'Can we check what time he left?'

'Sure.'

He asked the waitress if she could recall what they'd talked about, Mrs Lewis and her guest.

'No. But he gave her a book.'

'What kind of book?'

'I didn't see. He took the book from his little briefcase, and he wrote in it, and he gave it to her.'

Cupido didn't use the usual facilities for identification of the dead in the Salt River mortuary, as Vinnie Adonis was not a next of kin of Alicia Lewis. To save time he took the slightly anxious concierge straight to the refrigerators, apologising for the discomfort and strange smells, saying, 'It can be an unpleasant experience, uncle,' as he gave the official on duty the nod to open the drawer, and then to remove the white cloth.

Vinnie looked down with a blend of macabre curiosity and a sincere wish to make a correct identification. He had to step closer, lean over. He stood staring for a long time, till the urge to retch overcame him.

'The bucket is over there,' came the routine instruction from the bored mortuary assistant.

Adonis crouched over the bucket, but managed to control his nausea. With moist eyes he looked up at Cupido. 'It's her,' he said hoarsely.

'Uncle, are you sure?'

'Dead certain.'

Vaughn made the call to Benny.

★ ★ ★

Just before five in the afternoon, in the hotel manager's office, Griessel rang the London home number of Alicia Lewis.

He didn't pause to reflect on being the bearer of bad tidings again. He had played that role times without number in his job – from his days as a young constable in the northern suburbs conveying news of motorbike deaths to wives and mothers, to being the Hawks detective most often asked to break the news after a murder. 'You have the gravitas, Benna, the gravitas,' Cupido would say, trying to manipulate him.

It wasn't gravitas, it was experience. Far too much experience.

The phone rang in a house in London that he was unable to picture. It rang four, five, six times before someone answered: 'Hello?' The voice slightly out of breath.

'Good afternoon,' Griessel said, realising he had no idea what time it was in England. 'Who am I speaking to?'

'This is Tracy.'

'Madam, are you related to Mrs Alicia Lewis?'

'Miss Lewis. No. Why?'

'Is this her residence?'

'Yes. Who is this?'

'What is your relationship to Miss Lewis?'

'I'm sorry, who is this?'

'My name is Benny Griessel. I am a captain in the South African Police, I'm calling from Cape Town.'

'Oh, Jesus . . . Is Alicia okay?'

'May I ask what your relationship is to Miss Lewis, please?'

'I'm just her house-sitter. I . . . I'm a student, I . . . Is she okay?'

'Madam, I am very, very sorry to tell you that Miss Lewis passed away on Monday.' He kept his voice and tone gentle, because he knew these were words that changed people's lives forever.

Not gravitas. Just experience.

It took him five minutes to calm Tracy Williams down enough, alone there in that house in London, to ask her some questions.

She said for the past two years she had been looking after Lewis's house when she went on holiday, or was out of town for a weekend. At forty-three, Alicia Lewis had never been married, never had children. For the last few years she had had no romantic attachments. Lewis had a sister and a mother somewhere in America, 'I think Long Island or thereabouts . . .'

Could she find the contact details?

She would try . . .

Was there an employer who would have those details?

Yes, Restore ought to have them still. Lewis had resigned a month or so ago; she'd been with Restore for nearly twenty years. An art company.

Griessel asked whether Williams had contact numbers for the business.

No, but he could look up restore.art.co.uk, under 'Contact Us'.

He asked her what time it was in London.

Griessel was still on the phone with Lewis's former employer, taking down notes in his little book, when Cupido came in again. Vaughn carried both their murder cases, one in each hand. He put Griessel's down and went out again. Benny gathered that he was going to inspect Lewis's hotel room so long.

When he had completed the second phone call, Griessel picked up his case, and went to find the manager to thank him for allowing the SAPS to call overseas at the hotel's expense. Then he walked to room 202.

Cupido had stretched the yellow crime scene tape across the doorway. Vaughn's murder case – a big black attaché case like Griessel's – was on the floor in the passage, lid open. Beside it lay his long black winter coat and jacket, neatly folded. Griessel peered in at the door. Inside Cupido was kneeling beside the double bed, trying to peer underneath. On the bed was the dead woman's large suitcase, a bright turquoise blue. Vaughn was wearing blue hospital shoe covers and transparent latex gloves.

'I'm here,' said Griessel.

'PCSI are on the way,' said Cupido. He was referring to the elite Provincial Crime Scene Investigation Unit that frequently examined the Hawks' crime scenes.

'Okay.' Griessel put his case down beside the wall, took off his jacket and put it beside it. He took out the shoe protectors and gloves, and put them on. Then he ducked under the yellow tape, and entered the large hotel room. 'I called her house in London. There's no close family there, she has never married. There is a mother and a sister in America. I will call them, I'm just waiting for the phone numbers. Lewis lived alone. A girl, a student who is minding her house, said Lewis came to Cape Town on holiday. Lewis used to work at a place called Restore. They said she resigned at the end of March, and she wanted to take a year or two of sabbatical.'

'Now, a month ago?' Cupido straightened up and opened the travel case.

'Yes.'

'Sabbatical?'

'Yes, she—'

Cupido snorted. 'Sabbatical. I don't even know what that means. Imagine, a policeman saying, no, I'm a bit tired, I'm going to take a nice sabbatical. Or one of my coloured brothers: "Yes, my china, I'm taking a bit of sabbatical from my house painting job, maybe Mauritius . . ." Only rich white people throw that term around so other rich white people won't think they're lazy bums . . .'

Griessel knew it didn't help to interrupt Cupido when he was blowing off steam with one of his rants. He did it frequently and Benny suspected it was of great therapeutic value to his colleague. And for the most part it was amusing. Especially because he didn't consider Griessel 'white.' They had talked about that. Cupido said, 'Colour only applies to whites who have never suffered. You don't have colour, Benna.'

Griessel was never exactly sure what Vaughn meant by his 'suffering'. Probably the alcoholism.

He waited until his colleague was finished. 'She was in the arts. Big expert, they said, on old stuff. There's a woman who worked with her who was her best friend. They will ask her to call; at the moment she's in Europe somewhere. What have you done so far?'

'Taken photos of the whole room, and the contents of the wardrobe.' The detectives used their cell phones for that, if they were first on the scene. 'It's at the back there next to the bathroom, more like a walk-in closet. This is one grand hotel, Benna. Must cost a fortune. There are clothes and shoes, and a laptop in the top drawer, under her undies, like she was hiding it . . .'

'Maybe she thought it might be stolen.'

Cupido nodded. 'I called Lithpel, he'll wait at work until we bring it.' Sergeant Reginald 'Lithpel' Davids was the in-house tech genius for the Cape Hawks, attached to their Information Management Centre, or

IMC. 'So far, no passport,' said Cupido. 'No cell phone or charger . . .'

'Must be in her handbag,' said Griessel, because they could see on the CCTV material she had been carrying a fairly large bag over her shoulder when she left the hotel. 'Do we have the hired car's—' And then his cell phone rang.

He took it out, saw that it was Cloete calling, their media liaison officer. That meant the media had already heard that the Directorate for Priority Crimes had taken over the case. He didn't answer, he would call back later. He just said 'Cloete' when Cupido looked at him questioningly.

'The vultures are circling,' said Cupido.

9

Griessel inspected the hotel room for the first time. It was large and luxurious. The curtains of the French doors in the northern wall opened out onto a false balcony, with a view across the water, the yachts and the millionaires' apartment blocks on the Waterfront across the dock. The room had two easy chairs at a coffee table, a desk in classic style with a chair to match, an enormous double bed, perfectly made, two bedside cabinets and a large flat-screen TV.

'Tidy woman,' said Cupido. 'Only washing in the case.' He closed the turquoise suitcase, and carried it back to the large built-in wardrobe where he had found it.

Deon Meyer

'I'll check the bathroom,' said Griessel.

A bath, shower, two basins, all expensive, classy fittings. Snow-white towels, large and small, hung on hooks against the wall. Lewis's toiletry bag was between the washbasins. Cosmetics, toothpaste and a toothbrush were neatly arranged beside the hotel soaps, shampoo and shower gel. He inspected the toilet bag. Nothing out of the ordinary. He came back out of the bathroom.

Cupido pushed shut the drawer of a bedside cupboard. 'Nothing,' he said. 'Just the laptop.'

'Knock-knock.' A voice from the door. They recognised Jimmy, the tall, skinny one from PCSI.

'Who's there?' asked his forensic colleague Arnold – the short fat one – theatrically loud, for their benefit. The pair were nicknamed Thick and Thin, from the tired old joke that they themselves frequently told: PCSI will stand by you through Thick and Thin.

'Canoe,' said Jimmy.

'Canoe who?' asked Arnold.

'Canoe please help the Hawks? They're clueless.'

And then the pair roared with laughter as if it were the joke of the year.

Just before seven Griessel phoned Captain John Cloete, media liaison officer of the Hawks.

'What can you give me on the Bleached Body?' asked Cloete.

'The Bleached Body?'

'That's what the press call her.'

'She's an American citizen, John.'

Cloete sighed. That meant more fuss, even hysteria. Trouble. 'What else?'

'She arrived here as a tourist on Sunday. We've put a search out for her hired car,' and Griessel gave him the registration number. 'Anyone with information, the usual story . . .'

'That's all?'

'That's all that I want to share now.'

At 19:27 Griessel and Cupido jogged through the downpour of the first winter storm of the year. When they were on the way back to Bellville, Benny phoned Alexa. 'We're going to be late,' he said when she answered.

'What happened?' she asked with her usual concern.

'The Bleached Body.'

'I thought so. It was on the radio that the case had been sent to you. Have you found anything?'

'Nothing so far.'

'Shall I keep dinner for you?'

Alexa Barnard was an excellent businesswoman and still a brilliant singer. But cooking was not her strong point. She had no feel for it. Often she would be cooking while taking calls or answering emails, and not keep track of which ingredients she had added to the pot. Her sense of taste was also suspect. She would carefully taste a curry or pot of soup, declare it 'perfect', but when she dished up and began to eat she would frown and say, 'Something is not right now. Can you taste it too?'

So now he said, 'No thanks, we'll get something on the way.'

When he rang off, Cupido asked, 'She doesn't know anything about the engagement yet?'

'No.'

'Has the bank come back to you yet?'

'They're still thinking about it.'

'Maybe it's a sign, Benna.'

He laughed. 'You're just worried Desiree will hear we're engaged and then the pressure will be on you to make a plan.'

'Damn straight,' said Cupido. 'And it scares the shit out of me.'

Lithpel Davids was waiting in the large room of the DPCI's Information Management Centre, the IMC. He was small and fragile, with the face of a schoolboy, and a huge Afro hairstyle. He used to have a lisping speech impediment, until that was surgically corrected, but still, his nickname lived on.

Cupido handed him the Apple MacBook Pro, finger-print dust still visible on the silver surface.

'Come to papa,' said Lithpel, and began to rummage through his box of cables and chargers for the matching power point.

Cupido and Griessel sat down at the long table, opposite each other. As usual, during the drive, they had each considered the case; now they were ready to test theories. Griessel knew Cupido would begin.

'Okay, let me get this straight. My name is Alicia Lewis, I am forty-how-many years old?'

'Forty-three,' said Griessel.

'Forty-three. I worked with art for twenty years, give or take, and I was very wise, because I never got married' – casting a meaningful look at Griessel, who ignored his gaze – 'so I could save all my money, and now I'm taking a sabbatical . . .'

'Sabbat-what?' asked Lithpel Davids.

'Amen, brother, don't interrupt, the grown-ups are talking,' said Cupido.

'Grown-ups, my arse,' said Davids quietly.

'Okay, so I take a sabbatical, and what do I do?'

'I hang around for a month in London while I plan my first holiday,' said Griessel.

'Right. And of all the places in the universe that I can choose from, I come to the good old R of SA, specifically Cape Town. Which is fair enough, 'cause it's the most spectacularly beautiful city in the most awesome country on the planet. So far, so good.'

Griessel nodded.

'And the first thing I do after I get to the hotel, I ask the concierge how to get to Villiersdorp.'

'Villiersdorp?' said Lithpel Davids, his eyes on the screen of the MacBook, but clearly his ears not.

'Shurrup, Sergeant,' said Cupido. 'But that is exactly the point. Villiersdorp. Why Villiersdorp? With the utmost respect to the good people of Villiersdorp, that's not the first tourist destination that comes to mind if I'm a Yankee hanging out in Cape Town. Or am I completely missing the plot, Benna?'

'No, that was my first big question too. And her employer and house-sitter think that it's the very first time she's visited South Africa.'

'And your first order of business is breakfast with Grandpa? And your first special outing is to Villiersdorp? Curious.'

'Yip.'

'Who's Grandpa?' Davids asked. 'By the way, here's a bit of bad news. *This* aunty has a password on her user ID. It's going to take a little longer.'

'Grandpa is this ancient whitey uncle who shared Mrs Alicia Lewis's five-star breakfast feast with her, the very first morning she woke up in Cape Town.'

'*Aitsa*. Did he sleep over?' asked Davids.

'No, you pervert, he arrived in the morning all prim and proper.'

'But that means she had a date with him. So she knew him,' said Griessel.

'Obviously,' said Lithpel Davids.

'But that means maybe she didn't choose the Cape for its natural beauty, Sergeant. It means she had a different agenda, or an additional agenda.'

'Not necessarily,' said Griessel. 'Maybe Grandpa was an old friend in the arts.'

'True. But why have breakfast with him, first thing Monday morning, first morning of the holiday, when you still have two leisurely weeks ahead, just before you drive to Villiersdorp, never to be seen again.'

'That is the question,' said Griessel.

'And that's why Sergeant Slowly here has to open the laptop for us.'

'Have I ever failed you?'

Griessel's cell phone rang. It was Jimmy from Forensics. He answered. 'Jimmy?'

'I dare say, old boy, may I speak to Captain Ghreezel?' asked Jimmy with a fake British accent.

'She was an American, Jimmy. She worked in London.' He spoke with long-suffering patience in his voice; with Thick and Thin that was the only approach that worked.

'Oh,' said Jimmy, deflated. 'We wanted to let you know that there's not much here of use. No blood, no semen.

We'll take the cleaner's fingerprints tomorrow morning. Until then we can't say there are any unidentified fingerprints.'

'Thanks, Jimmy.'

'Y'all have a good night, now,' he said in an exaggerated American accent.

Lithpel Davids sat back in his chair, entwined his fingers and said, 'There you go, password cracked. So what do you need from this baby?'

IO

'We want to know why she came to Cape Town. Why she wanted to go to Villiersdorp,' said Griessel. 'Anything . . .'

'The usual stuff. Check her email, her Facebook and her calendar,' said Cupido.

'I read you, Captain, I read you . . .'

'She didn't . . . The thing about the holiday . . . What bothers me most, is the bleach,' said Griessel.

'I know,' said Cupido. 'It's sort of contradictory.'

'That's a big word for a policeman,' said Davids while doing things on the MacBook screen. 'Why is the bleach contradictory?'

'How much bleach do you carry around in your car, Lithpel?'

'None.'

'Exactly.'

'I'm not following.'

'So here comes this dolly from England, the first chance she gets she takes a rental to an obscure, unimportant little town a hundred kilos outside Cape Town . . .'

'We suspect . . .' said Griessel.

'Or in that general direction. And she happens to run into a guy with a truckload of bleach who wants to kill her? Pure coincidence?'

'But he could have capped her first, and then gone to buy the bleach,' said Lithpel.

'That's the point,' said Griessel. 'It doesn't fit.'

''Causewhy,' said Cupido, 'this looks like a very organised killer. With this sort of thing . . . Okay, it's more the serial killer thing, but consider for a moment, if you will, the facts of this specific case; the way the body was presented, like a window dressing, very structured. It has the whiff of a serial killer type of murder. We don't say it is, we just say there is—'

'Food for thought,' said Griessel.

'What he said,' Cupido agreed. 'Now, in this sort of thing you get your organised killers, your disorganised killers, and you get some that are a mix between the two. But this guy: one blow, just one blow to kill her, clean, efficient. Businesslike. Very organised. Careful washing of the body in bleach. Very clever, very organised. He takes her clothes, her handbag, her car, her phone, everything, he dumps it all somewhere. Smart. Organised. Carefully displays the body on this little wall in a pretty public place. A place where he knows someone will find her. That's what he wants. Again, very organised.'

'Not the sort of ou who would murder her on the spur of the moment, and then start running around buying bleach,' said Griessel.

'Contradictory,' said Cupido.

'Clutching at straws,' said Lithpel Davids. 'Sounds like you guys don't have much to go on.'

Griessel nodded. 'That's true. But that's why we have to know what her plans were on Monday. And who knew about them.'

'I'll do what I can,' said Sergeant Lithpel Davids. 'But it is going to take a while. She didn't configure an email client. Which means she did email in her browser. Now the question is, what web mail, and do we need a password?'

They let Davids get on with his work, while they went to Griessel's office to broaden the search for the missing hired car to a province-wide alert, and to update the case file.

At 22:48 Griessel's cell phone rang. He saw that it was an overseas number, and said, 'I think it's her friend.'

He answered the call: 'This is Captain Griessel.'

'Hello. My name is Carol Coutts.' She spoke with a broad Scottish accent, resonating with emotion. 'Alicia Lewis was my best friend.'

Carol Coutts sounded like a strong woman. First he asked, 'Can I call you back?' and she said, no, thank you, and then, with a tremor in her voice: 'I want to know how she died.' He told her, as tactfully as possible, the outlines of what they knew. She wasn't crying yet, but asked, 'Do you have suspects?' and 'Do you have leads?'

She also did not cry when Griessel began to answer her. She told him that Lewis was a very intelligent woman, earning an MA in Classical and Antique Art from Arizona State University, and later a post-graduate diploma in the UK.

'She worked at the Art Loss Register in London for seven years, as Recoveries Case Manager.'

'I'm sorry, I don't know what that is, the Art Loss Register.'

'It's an international . . . As a matter of fact, it's the biggest private database of lost and stolen art in the world. They . . . If your art is stolen, they'll search for it, and try to recover it. She worked on the recovery side, she was very good. That's why Restore head-hunted her.'

'That's where you worked together? At this company, Restore?'

'Yes, for more than ten years.'

'What does Restore do?'

'It's quite similar to ... Well, to be honest, we're in direct competition to the Art Loss Register, like several other companies. We have our own database, and we offer a very comprehensive service on all aspects of recovering works of art and collectables that are lost or stolen.'

'Madam, this must be a stupid question, but I need to understand: how do you "lose" a valuable piece of art?'

'No, it's a valid question. There ... For instance, thousands of families lost art worth billions of dollars during the Second World War, because of displacement, or the Nazis. And then there are natural disasters, art theft, art ransom, there are so many ways art can get lost.'

'And Restore, they find the art again?'

'Well, we try, but it's more than that. We assist our clients with research, for instance on the legal title of a piece of art, we provide dispute resolution, or advice on potential claims. And of course the recovery services, where Alicia and I worked.'

'What exactly did she do?'

Griessel knew how unpredictable the effects of loss and grief could be, how they were triggered by different memories. He was not at all taken aback when she began to sob. He waited patiently, saying, 'I'm so sorry.' He let her cry, surprised at the sudden impulse he felt to put out a hand to comfort her.

Eventually she was able to tell him how she and Alicia Lewis managed the process of recovering lost or stolen art – and other collectibles of high value. It involved her having an initial interview with the client, and then setting in motion all the necessary actions – liaising with insurers and law enforcement, sometimes private investigators, the people or institutions that had the artwork in their possession, museums and experts that could verify the genuine article – to trace the item, to make sure the client's claims to ownership were valid, and to enforce those claims and rights. 'It really is all in the title. We are Recoveries Case Managers, with the emphasis on "managers."'

'Did she have contact with people in South Africa?'

'I . . . Perhaps. I don't . . .'

He could hear she was struggling again. 'Should I call you tomorrow, ma'am?'

'No . . . I'm sorry . . . There wasn't any case file that I'm aware . . . Do you mean professionally, did she know someone professionally in South Africa?'

'Or personally. Did she ever talk about people in South Africa, in Cape Town, that she knew, or wanted to visit?'

'No . . . Not that . . . I'm sorry . . .'

'Did she talk about coming to South Africa on holiday?'

The line was silent, he could hear only her breathing, so many thousands of kilometres away. He heard her sniff, and blow her nose, take a deep breath and say, 'You know, Captain, she never did. We were . . . I'm almost fifty years old, I'm not naive or overly sentimental, and I think I'm pretty realistic when it comes to friendship . . . any relationship, for that matter. So when I tell you we were the best of friends, I'm not exaggerating. It was such a . . . a comfortable friendship. Like an old gown, we used to joke, cosy and warm and soft and familiar when you needed it, but all was well even if it was hung up in the wardrobe for a while. No demands, no expectations, just . . . easy. She had always been single, I've been divorced for thirteen years now, we had other friends, we had different interests, but for the past decade, we saw each other just about every working day, we had lunch together two, three times a week, and most of all, I believed we had no secrets from each other. We would talk about absolutely everything. And I mean everything. I always thought the most valuable thing about our friendship was the trust.

'And then, at the end of February . . . Actually, to be honest, it was a little before that. In . . . In January, something changed. I don't know what it was, it was just . . . She was . . . I know this sounds silly, but it was as if she was looking away, as if her gaze had lifted to a . . . horizon of sorts, another horizon. I didn't really react at the time, you know, I thought she might have met someone, or maybe . . . we all go through phases, and I . . . But then, at the end of February, she came into my office and she sat down and she said, Carol, I've had enough. I'm going to resign. Completely out of the blue, I never saw it coming, I had no idea she was . . . that she had had enough, as she put it. Never, ever, did she say a word to me that she was unhappy, I always thought she enjoyed the work. Anyway, I felt a bit betrayed, the trust thing . . . Just like I feel now. You know we had brunch together, the Saturday before last, and all she said to me was that she was thinking of going away for a while, and I asked where, and she said, maybe Spain, she hadn't made up her mind yet. But she never breathed a word about South Africa.'

It was half past eleven when Griessel drove home in the rain to Brownlow Street, Oranjezicht, and tiptoed up the stairs as quietly as possible. He showered in the spare bathroom so as not to disturb Alexa. All the while the Alicia Lewis case occupied his thoughts.

In the chill of the bathroom he stood naked and ready to step into the shower when his cell phone sounded a text notification. It was Lithpel Davids: *Gmail, no auto-login. Will take time. Going to zzzz.*

He put down the phone, got into the shower and opened the taps. His thoughts flowed with the water. He saw the way she died. One awful blow to the back of her head. One moment alive, the next just gone. All her secrets, her new horizons, gone with her into eternity.

One terrible blow to the back of her head.

You needed room to swing a pipe like that. She would have to be standing still, her attention somewhere else; it wasn't a frontal assault, so she wasn't expecting it.

Why?

He got out, towelled dry. He turned off the lights, walked quietly to bed, climbed in, hearing the rain beating down on the roof. Alexa's body was warm, her arms welcoming and she snuggled up to him and sighed in contentment. 'Love you,' she said from somewhere in her sleep. That's why he wanted to marry her, he thought. Coming home to this. *She* was his home.

But how could you explain that to Vaughn Cupido?

11

Saturday morning, still dark at 6:24, the N1 almost free of traffic. Griessel was driving to work when his cell phone rang, not a number he recognised. He answered it.

'Captain, this is Sergeant Duba, Somerset West.'

'Good morning, Sergeant.'

'Morning, Captain. I've just had a call from a Professor Wilke, who was listening to the radio, and he heard that you have identified the Bleached Body. He says he had breakfast with her on Monday morning. He got hold of Wednesday's newspaper article online, the one with my contact details, so he called me. Can I text you the professor's telephone number?'

Griessel phoned the professor from his car, heard the man answer with 'Hello, this is Professor Marius Wilke,' and he wondered why it was so important for some people to have a title, and to use it. He seldom used his own with the public, only if it was an official discussion – and absolutely necessary.

He made use of it now, a little self-consciously: 'This is Captain Benny Griessel.' He asked where the professor was, because they wanted to come and talk to him about his meeting with Alicia Lewis.

'I'm in Schonenberg, here in Somerset West, but listen, the trouble is, I don't know how much I can say. I mean, if I can tell you everything Ms Lewis and I talked about. I'll have to make sure.'

In his imagination Griessel connected the high, somewhat hoarse voice on the phone to the dapper figure on the hotel CCTV cameras and it made him smile. Comical little man. The sort that would give Vaughn Cupido more grist for his mill.

'How so?'

'I signed a contract, Benny.' Like they were old friends. 'And my word is my honour.'

★   ★   ★

He said nothing to his colleague about the professor's mannerisms. They drove to Somerset West just after seven, the sun not yet risen, the mountains behind Gordon's Bay etched black against the slowly lightening horizon. At the Schonenberg Retirement Village they had to stop at a boom and sign the register. The security guard said he would phone 'the Prof' to check that they had an appointment.

'We are the Hawks, my bru, we don't need an appointment,' said Cupido.

'Just humour me, brother, I'm only doing my job.' That was a language Cupido understood. He nodded, and the guard phoned, opened the gate, and gave them directions. They drove past the rows of neat little houses, black roofs, pale yellow walls and manicured gardens. Two women came down the road, power-walking with exaggerated, purposeful swinging of arms in the morning half-light.

Griessel parked in front of Wilke's house and got out. The door opened, and the little man came out, dressed formally in a brown tweed jacket, white shirt and bluish-grey tie, his snowy hair still damp, but perfectly combed. 'Morning, morning, morning, gentlemen.' He thrust out his hand to Cupido who was nearest. 'Professor Marius Wilke, pleased to meet you, pleased to meet you.' He was even smaller, busier and more dapper than the video suggested, a caricature with a big nose and high-pitched voice, radiating cheeriness, with twinkling eyes and *joie de vivre*.

He pumped each detective's hand vigorously, repeating their names and ranks multiple times, perhaps to commit them to memory, and invited them inside. 'Coffee? I have a pot on the go, filter coffee, good coffee, how does that sound?'

The kitchen, dining and sitting areas formed a single open-plan unit, crammed bookshelves lined every wall and the many windows conspired to make it attractive, yet at the same time homely and dignified.

They said what they wanted, he nodded his approval and rattled on while he organised the cups. He described his shock that morning when he'd heard on the radio news that the Bleached Body's name was Alicia Lewis. He listened to the early news every morning on the radio; the trouble with getting old, one didn't sleep as much, so he would be awake before dawn waiting for the six o'clock bulletin. The other morning, the news about the body in Sir Lowry's Pass, later the talk about bleach, and you didn't expect it, you simply didn't expect to know the murdered one, the victim. That poor, poor woman. And he had breakfast with her Monday morning, such a pleasant breakfast, she is . . . he meant she *was*, in person, so much nicer than in the emails and telephone conversations . . .

The professor came around the corner of the kitchen carrying a tray of steaming mugs and a plate of rusks. 'Help yourselves, help yourselves, Benny, may I call you Benny? I did get hold of my lawyer, after I talked to you, just to make sure about the confidentiality clause, and he said I can talk to you, as it *is* a murder investigation. So I phoned you back straight away, because I know, all the crime programmes on TV, the first seventy-two hours are crucial, hmm . . .?'

'What confidentiality clause?' asked Cupido.

'Old Vaughn, *jong*, it's quite an interesting story. Very interesting . . .' And Marius Wilke suddenly sprang to his feet and crossed the floor to a bookshelf. 'You see, all my life I've been a historian here at the university' – with a vague wave in the direction of Stellenbosch – 'History Department, of course.' And he took four thick tomes off the shelf and brought them back, offering them to Cupido. 'This is my life's work, apart from the academic papers, naturally, this is my life's work, the history of the Cape, from 1600 to 1900, broadly, broadly speaking; it was my life's work, my passion, four books, translated into seven languages, published in sixteen countries.'

Cupido took the books from him, inspected the titles, and passed them on to Griessel.

'But when I retired, seven years ago, can you believe it, it was seven years ago, I'm turning seventy-three' – and the professor sat down again opposite them – 'then for fun I began researching the family history of the Wilkes, but thorough research, *jong*. I have the knowledge, and you know how it works, you talk about it, and people say they also want to research their genealogies like that, but they don't know how and they don't have the time. So you say, let me help because I like scratching around in the archives, and before you realise it you have a business, because people pay for your research services, and you gain a reputation and it just grows. And naturally, because you are a professor, because you publish, you have an *oeuvre*, you're known, people trust you, people know they're getting the real McCoy. They know, if you say *this* is their genealogy, then it *is*. And my grandson made me a website, and the business grew big, old Vaughn, you won't believe how busy I was in my retirement, but I made some good money, and could pick and choose, such a privilege, to be able to pick and choose what projects you take on . . .'

The professor stopped to take a breath and a sip of coffee. Griessel and Cupido were silent. Instinctively they didn't want to break the man's momentum; there was something captivating about the way the hoarse voice and nose and the lively eyes together with the childlike body generated energy, like a small dynamo.

'Good, good,' said Marius Wilke. 'So in July last year I received an email via the website, did I tell you, it's at www.yourheritage.co.za? That's the name of my website, you can take a look, my grandson set it up. So I received the email from Alicia Lewis, and she asked if I was the author of *Good Hope, 1488 to 1806*, that's the English translation of my third book. And I replied and said, indeed, indeed, and she asked me, do I do freelance research, and I said indeed, indeed. So she sent me the contract, and right near the beginning . . . Wait, let me get it, just a second, it's on my desk, the contract, the confidentiality clause,' and he jumped up again, an aged jack-in-the-box in a brown tweed jacket, and he disappeared down the passage.

'Donald Duck,' whispered Vaughn Cupido, with a grin and Griessel had to suppress a guffaw: the description was so spot-on, the voice, the nose, the waddling, dapper, cocky walk, a cockalorum, a cartoon duck. But he was back again, document in hand, and Benny choked back his laughter and watched the professor place the document carefully on the coffee table.

Wilke said Alicia Lewis had made him sign this first, which naturally piqued his curiosity, who wouldn't be curious, hey old Vaughn, if someone told you there was a big secret? I mean, I'm a historian, unravelling secrets is my business, my passion.

So he signed, and she phoned him immediately, here in this house, and told him, Prof, I want you to go to the Cape Archives for me and search for a reference to a painting by Carel Fabritius.

The prof said the name 'Carel Fabritius!' like the ring-side announcer at a boxing match who knew he would arouse tumultuous applause.

An awkward, deathly silence followed. The detectives had not the slightest clue what the professor meant, they had never heard of Fabritius.

'Who?' asked Cupido.

'Fabritius,' said the professor emphatically, but with less sense of fanfare, his expectations dampened.

'We don't know who that is,' said Griessel.

'*The Goldfinch*?' said the professor, still hopeful.

They both shook their heads.

'Donna Tartt?' queried the professor, but you could tell he knew by now what their response would be.

Their blank faces showed they had never heard of her.

'You have heard of Rembrandt?'

'Of course.' Cupido brightened. 'Everyone's heard of Rembrandt.'

'Good, now Carel Fabritius was one of Rembrandt's pupils. To tell the truth, he was the only one of Rembrandt's pupils who really developed a style of his own. If you ask me, he was the best of Rembrandt's pupils.'

'So he's dead already?'

'Yes, of course . . .'

'Okay, Prof, let's cut to the chase,' said Cupido. 'Why is it a big thing that she asked you about this?'

'Well, first, there are only a couple of Fabritius paintings left around the world, and the possibility that there might be one in South Africa . . . That is phenomenal. But there's more, much more. I went to search the archives. And I found a reference. A reliable, trusted source, who referred to a Fabritius painting, here in the Cape.'

12

'Cool,' said Vaughn Cupido. 'And who has the painting?'

'Gysbert van Reenen,' said the professor.

'Do you have an address?' said Griessel, taking out his notebook and starting to make notes.

Marius Wilke chuckled, a sound so like the quacking of a duck that Griessel and Cupido could not help laughing too.

'I have an address,' said Wilke when he calmed down. 'Papenboom in Newlands. There is only one problem. You are two and a quarter centuries late.'

They just stared at him.

'The reference to a Fabritius painting was made by Louis Michel Thibault in 1788,' said Wilke.

The detectives frowned again.

'Thibault is the one the Thibault Square in the city is named after . . .'

'Aah,' said Benny Griessel.

'Okay,' said Vaughn Cupido.

'Thibault was an architect, an influential, wonderful man; it was he who . . . Do you know Groot Constantia, those glorious gables?'

The detectives nodded.

'Well, it's believed that those were Thibault's work. Very interesting man. A Frenchman, highly cultivated, highly educated, and brave too. He was a soldier when he arrived in the Cape in 1783, but okay, okay, you don't want a lecture now, eh? The important thing is that Alicia Lewis asked me to search for any possible reference to a painting by Fabritius, and I thought it would be a waste of time, but she paid in pounds sterling, and one does not say no to that, not with this exchange rate. And can you believe it, I found it. In 1788. Thibault, who designed and built a house for Gysbert van Reenen on Papenboom in Newlands. Thibault wrote about it in his journal: he was at the house-warming celebration, and hanging on the wall was this astonishingly beautiful painting, and the name at the bottom was C. Fabritius, and the year 1654. Can you believe it? A Fabritius! In the Cape! That is phenomenal.'

The detectives nodded, but without enthusiasm.

Griessel looked up from his notebook: 'In 1788?'

'Yes,' said Wilke, with passionate amazement.

'Prof, is that what you were talking about on Monday over breakfast? About something that was written hundreds of years ago in a dead oke's diary?' Cupido asked.

'Among other things. Oh, it was such a stimulating discussion, she was a fascinating woman, so interesting. Oh, I took her one of my books, incidentally, a copy to sign just for her, she was a very good client . . .'

'And that's all?' Griessel asked.

'No, not entirely. I wanted to know if she had traced the painting, if she had followed up the names that I had given her.'

'What names?'

'That's the thing, old Benny, that's the thing. Thibault wrote in his diary that the Fabritius painting had been in the van Reenen family for a few generations already. Over a hundred years. Oubaas van Reenen told him it always went to the oldest son. That was all in the report that I wrote for Alicia. She came back to me immediately, asked me to make a family tree. I had to try to track down Gysbert van Reenen's descendants. Now why would she want to do that, old Vaughn? Why? She wanted to find out where the painting is now, I am sure of it.'

'And who does have the painting now?' Cupido asked impatiently. In his opinion Donald Duck could have come to the point a long time ago.

'I don't know,' said Professor Marius Wilke. 'The problem is, primogeniture is not always straightforward. Sometimes the eldest son dies before the parents, there aren't always sons in the paternal line; a number of things can confuse the matter. I sent her nine possible names, of people who are alive, direct descendants of the old Gysbert van Reenen, who might have inherited. If no one has sold it, of course.'

'And then?'

'She said thank you very much, and she paid me. I told her, if she ever came to South Africa, she should let me know, and I would give her one of my books, signed of course, since she was my very best client, and not shy to pay. For months I heard nothing, but just last week, I received an email, and she invited me to breakfast in that wonderful hotel.'

'And she told you who has the painting now?'

The professor's face fell. 'No. That was a great disappointment to me. She said it seemed as though the painting . . . as though it had disappeared.'

They digested this information.

'And that's it?'

'Well, at least we had a wonderful discussion, about art and history. She is a very intelligent woman, well read and well travelled and highly cultivated. Highly cultivated.'

'And then?'

'Then I came home, and I went on with my work. But then I heard the news of her passing this morning.'

They processed this information, disappointed.

'Did she say where she was going, on Monday? Who she wanted to see?'

'No, not that I can remember. She said she just wanted to explore the Cape, and my book was going to make it a very special experience.'

'Did she say anything about Villiersdorp?'

'Villiersdorp?'

'That's right.'

The professor thought a while. 'No. Not at all . . .'

'Did she mention any other appointments? People she knew in South Africa?'

'No. Nothing.'

Griessel rose reluctantly. He had hoped for more. Then something occurred to him: 'Were any of the names, those nine names that you gave her, were any of them in Villiersdorp?'

'Old Benny, no, you don't understand. She only asked me for the names, the full names and ID numbers if I could get them. I didn't . . . I am not geared for finding people, addresses and such. I don't even drive any more . . .'

'May we have the names, in any case?'

The professor picked up the document from the coffee table and passed it to Griessel. 'It's all here,' he said. 'The contract, the confidentiality clause, and the names. I can get the research material for you too, of course.'

Griessel took the document.

Cupido stood up. 'Prof, what do you estimate a Fictitious painting like that is worth?' he asked.

'Fabritius,' said Wilke.

'That one,' said Cupido.

'That's exactly what I asked her. She said it depends on the condition of the painting. And if it really exists, and if it is genuine. She said it's impossible to put a value on it, it's "priceless," that's the word she used. So I asked her, what if something like that went on auction, at Christie's, what did she think it would sell for. And she said, at least fifty million.'

'Shoo,' said Griessel.

'Dollars,' said the professor.

'*Slaat my* . . .' said Cupido.

'But probably closer to a hundred million.'

'*Jissis*,' said Griessel and Cupido in unison.

He accompanied them to their car. 'Are you going to catch the people who . . .?' and he motioned in the direction of the mountains and the pass.

'We'll do our very best, Professor.'

'You must hurry, old Benny, you must hurry. Before someone smuggles that painting out of the country.'

They drove the first stretch of the road back to work in silence, taking the N2 and then the R300, while they pondered the new information.

At last Griessel said, with an air of resignation, 'Funny old world . . .'

'Damn straight,' said Cupido. 'Hundred million dollars . . .'

'A quarter of a century in the SAPS, and I can't even scrape together twenty-two thousand rand to buy an engagement ring, not even if I sell my bass guitar and my amp. But there are people who can cough up that sort of money for a painting . . .'

'A picture, Benna. That painting is just a picture. A few brush strokes and a pot of paint. By a dead Dutchman.'

'A hundred million *dollars*.'

'One and a half billion rand. That's just obscene.' And then, suddenly worried: 'You're not going to do that, Benna, are you?'

'What?'

'Sell your bass guitar.'

'No. I can't afford to, because then I lose the thousand two hundred I make from the gigs with the band. I thought, if I can save that money, I can buy the ring in five months . . .'

Cupido sighed deeply. Life was totally unfair.

13

They took the Strand off-ramp. Saturday night traffic had woken up, parking for the factory shops at Access City was chock-a-block already.

At the Stikland Cemetery Griessel said, 'There's one thing that keeps bothering me . . .'

'What?'

Griessel took a moment to gather his thoughts. 'At Murder and Robbery, one of my first cases . . . It must be nearly twenty years back, when we were still in Bellville South . . . Anyway, I was on a case, the body of a con man by the name of Volmink had been found in the President

Hotel in Parow. Three or four stab wounds. That was the first time I heard about the pirate-map scam – that fake old map that is supposed to show where the big treasure is buried . . .'

Cupido knew it, he just nodded and said, 'X marks the spot . . .'

'That's right. Volmink was doing a version of that, spreading the myth of an old English ship that sank on the west coast with lots of gold. He had just about convinced a pig farmer from Kraaifontein to invest in the "expedition," but he drank and talked too much that night in the President bar, and one of his drinking buddies also believed the map was genuine, and later on knocked on his door with a knife . . .'

'You think this story of Prof Donald Duck is a treasure-map scam?'

'I . . . No . . . It just feels that way, Vaughn. A hundred million dollars? That doesn't sound right. For a painting by a man I've never heard of? And the coincidence . . . What did Prof Duck say? There are only a couple of his paintings left in the world. What are the chances that one would be in South Africa? I mean . . .'

'I hear you. Do you think Donald is in on the scam?'

'No. But with the Volmink case, back then . . . They, the swindlers, they talk about the first stage of the con as the "foundation work," when they lay the ground-work, when they build credibility. Volmink bought a genuine antique map, on an auction somewhere, the map *was* old. It was part of his foundation work; the con worked better if you had something genuine to show. Maybe Alicia Lewis got Prof Duck to provide credibility, without him knowing what her plans were. He had to find her something that really did happen. Perhaps she already knew about the historical reference, maybe she just wanted him to . . . I don't know . . .' And he suddenly doubted his theory.

'No, Benna, you might just be on to something. This aunty works for the great art recovery company, every day she sees them pay crazy prices for pictures, and she schemes, these rich bums are all so gullible, so eager, let's create a myth, a painting worth a hundred million dollars . . .'

'And then someone thought it really did exist . . .'

'Exactly . . .'

'But if you think the painting is genuine, and if you think only Lewis knows where it is, why kill her with a single blow, and leave her body on the pass?'

'Shit . . .'

They decided to call Carol Coutts again. They could carefully enquire about the possibility of a swindle. They sat in Griessel's office both listening to the call. She sounded half-asleep when she answered, and Griessel realised he'd forgotten about the time difference again.

He apologised profusely, but she said please, no, she was usually awake much earlier. But the news of the death of her friend had caused her a bad night's sleep.

Griessel introduced Cupido to her over the phone. Then he said that they had fresh information on the case and would like to test her opinion, but they didn't have to talk now if this was a bad time.

No, she said. She really did want to help. She needed clarity. The secret that Alicia Lewis apparently had kept from her was one of the things keeping her awake.

By turns they related the morning's events. Every now and then they had to ask if she was still there, and she just said, 'Yes.'

When they had described all the information from their visit to Prof Marius Wilke, there was dead silence over the phone.

'Are you there?' Cupido asked.

'Yes.'

They waited. She said nothing. Cupido didn't handle silences well. He filled this one by very carefully telling her about their theory, of the possibility of a scam, specifically about the treasure-map con.

'No,' she said with absolute certainty. And then she started to cry, and she apologised, and kept on crying. 'Just a minute,' she said. They could hear, far away in a bedroom somewhere in Europe, how she put the phone down on something, and then it was quiet, and then they heard her blow her nose, twice, the rustle of her picking up the phone and apologising once again.

Then she said, 'This is actually a huge relief. Somehow. At least I know what she was doing. If she believed the Fabritius was real, there is a very, very good chance that it does exist. You see, that period, those painters, the Baroque and Dutch Golden Era painters . . . She was one of the true experts. Especially when it came to lost works. And . . . It's just that her relationship with art . . . She would never . . . I just don't think she would. I don't know, Captain, perhaps I didn't know her as well as I thought, but my gut tells me this was definitely not a scam.'

Cupido couldn't restrain himself any longer. He asked if things like that really still happened, old, antique paintings found that were worth something.

Carol Coutts make a sound, and then she said, 'Oh, yes,' and she told them about the missing Gauguin still-life that was discovered in the American state of Connecticut barely a year ago. 'It sold for more than a million dollars . . .'

'But that's the point, ma'am,' said Cupido. 'This professor was telling us the Fabritius will sell for a hundred million dollars, which is just ridiculous.'

Not at all, Coutts said. In 2014 a Frenchman climbed into the attic of his old country home just outside Toulouse to mend a leaking water pipe, and came down with a painting that was identified in April 2016 as a masterpiece by the Italian painter Caravaggio. The whole art world expected it to sell for more than a hundred and twenty million dollars. 'Gauguin's picture of two Tahitian girls sold for three hundred million dollars in 2015,' she said. '*The Card Players* by Paul Cézanne went for almost two hundred and eighty million. Picasso's *Les Femmes d'Alger* sold for a hundred and seventy-nine million dollars . . .'

'*Jissis*,' said Cupido.

'That French guy who found the painting in the attic, who'll get the money when it's sold?' Griessel asked.

'The Frenchman,' said Carol Coutts. 'I know the "hidden fortune in the attic" sounds like a scam, like a fairy tale. But it happens. And more often than you think. Have you heard of the Munich artworks?'

'No,' they said in unison.

'In February 2012, German police found more than one thousand three hundred lost works of art in an apartment in Munich. They included works by Monet and Renoir and Matisse.'

Some of the names sounded familiar. 'Cool,' said Cupido, and then his phone rang, and he saw it was Sergeant Lithpel Davids. 'Sorry,' he said, silencing his phone.

Coutts seemed not to notice the interruption. She said, 'So, here's what I . . . I think Alicia . . . I think what happened was that something came across her desk. Something about the Fabritius. Some sort of . . . lead. Like when a detective . . . You know. I mean, in a certain sense, we're also detectives. We gather clues. We often have other people investigate them, but . . . I think she got some sort of lead, and I think it was a solid lead. Solid enough for her to . . .

'Look, she didn't like to talk about it, but her sister . . . Alicia's mother is in the US. The mom's been suffering from dementia for a while now, and her sister is a . . . let's just say she's a bit of a loose cannon. Prefers not to work too much, I gathered. So Alicia's been taking care of her mother financially, and you know how it is with medical costs, and speciality care, it's outrageously expensive. I just think Alicia saw an opportunity to pursue something . . . in a more personal regard. Something that would've made good money. I mean, I've thought about it, we've all thought about it in this profession . . . Maybe she was really struggling financially.'

'So you honestly think this is genuine?'

'The Fabritius? I'm sure of it.'

'Why?'

'Because Alicia was one of three international experts on that era. And she was sceptical and smart and not easily fooled.'

They went to Lithpel Davids in the IMC room. When they entered the sergeant said, 'The bad news is I can't open Alicia Lewis's email. If we had her phone . . . But on the laptop I just can't crack it. Cappie, she's using some heavy-duty password, so it's going to take a few days.'

'Shit,' said Cupido. 'And the good news? Tell me there's some good news.'

'I know who she had breakfast with on Monday morning.' Quite smug.

'Professor Marius Wilke?'

'Damn, how did you know that?'

'We detect, Lithpel, that's our job. How did you know?'

'It was in her calendar, and the prof's email and telephone and web address was in her contacts. So you know about the PI too?'

'What PI?'

'Haven't you been detecting, Cappie?'

'What PI, Sergeant?'

'The one in Claremont . . .'

'Claremont. Our Claremont? Southern suburbs?'

'Damn straight, Captain. Our Claremont.'

'Who's the PI?'

'Billy de Palma.'

Cupido made a peculiar sound in his throat. Griessel looked at him. His colleague's face was rigid and pale.

'Do you know him?' he asked.

'*Jirre*, Benna,' said Cupido, his voice muted. Then Vaughn looked at Davids: 'Tell me you're kidding me.'

'I kid thee not, come look here.' And he pointed at the MacBook. The detectives went closer. Davids pointed at the screen. In Alicia Lewis's contacts application was the entry for Billy de Palma Private Investigations, then the web address, email address and a cell phone number.

'Who is Billy de Palma?' Griessel asked. He could see Cupido was upset.

'How did you find that?' Cupido asked Davids.

'I can also detect, Cappie,' said Davids. 'I just searched through her contacts for dot za emails and for plus-twenty-seven telephone country codes and there he was. Billy de Palma. And the professor of course. Only two South Africans in her database, as far as I can see.'

'Billy de fokken Palma,' said Cupido, his hands on the edge of the desk, knuckles white.

'Who is Billy de Palma?' Griessel repeated patiently.

'He's the one who's killed Alicia Lewis, Benna,' said Cupido. He walked to the door, halted, turned back. 'He's a fucking psychopath, I'm telling you. I think we better go and see Major Mbali. Now.'

14

Griessel pacified Cupido first, got him to calm down. He said, 'Who is this guy?'

'Maybe you know him, Benna, but Billy de Palma isn't his real name. That's just what he calls his company: Billy de Palma Private Investigations. It's camouflage. Remember the ANC bigwig, former Deputy Premier of the Western Cape that they caught DUI, seven, eight years back? The one who nearly broke the breathalyser record for inebriation, he drove a Porsche Cayenne, *lekka* on the gravy train . . .'

'Tony somebody . . .'

'That's the one. Tony Dimaza. Remember how they lost the evidence of the DUI, here at the SAPS station Cape Town?'

'Vaguely.' Because that was during a phase when Griessel had been drunk all the time.

'All fingers pointed to a detective called Martin Fillis, remember him?'

'Sounds familiar . . .'

'Martin Reginald Fillis. Fillis. Piece of work. Piece of shit. Narcissist, psycho, real arsehole. We go way back. I was still wet behind the ears at the Drug Squad, he was my senior, already an inspector. From the start, I didn't like him. Creepy, I don't know, he had those eyes, Benna, there's no life there. And everyone says, you don't mess with him, he's a big ou, and some sort of martial arts expert who fights in a cage on weekends. Anyway, back then, prostitute turns up at Seapoint charge office, black and blue, some sick fuck had worked her over really badly and she wanted to lay a charge. It was Fillis who beat her like that when she refused to give him a freebie. Who beats up a woman like that?' Griessel could see that Cupido was reliving events that upset him, but he shrugged off the memory and said, 'In any case, Fillis had an alibi; one or other of his civilian buddies swore blind that they'd been together. Nothing happened, but a lot of us knew it was him.

'Then a few years later, when Fillis was a detective at Caledon Square, it was the Tony Dimaza thing, DUI evidence just disappeared. Fillis was the main suspect. Someone saw him in the evidence lock-up, and he couldn't explain a twenty-thousand deposit in his bank account, and his cell phone showed that he took a call from Dimaza two days before the evidence disappeared; they gave him a full investigation and a disciplinary hearing. I think the Service really wanted to be shot of him, and he knew he wasn't going to get off, so he saved everyone the embarrassment and resigned. Then he went and set up a PI business. And, because he was ashamed of his perfectly decent coloured surname, and because he was afraid his bad reputation would catch up with him, and most likely 'cause he probably wanted to sound fancy and white and Continental, he called his company Billy de Palma Private Investigations. He couldn't get a licence here in the Cape, they say he had to get one in the Free State, from his corrupt politician buddies.'

'Okay,' said Griessel. 'But how do we know that he's the murderer of Alicia Lewis?'

'Number one: one strike with a pipe, Benna. One very hard blow. It takes a big ou, a fast and strong ou. One who can hit, because he did martial arts, for years. Number two: body washed in bleach. That shows it's an ou who knows forensics, about DNA and blood and chemicals. Like an ou who was a detective in the SAPS. Number three: there's his name in Alicia Lewis's contacts. The only PI on the continent to have that honour. Number four: what do you do when Professor Donald Duck gives you nine names of potential owners of a very expensive painting, but you're sitting in London, and you want those nine people traced? You get yourself a private eye. You Google private investigators, and you contact the one who looks reputable, and you say, go find these people. And that's what he did. He found the nine, and he pinpointed the one with the painting, and that's why she resigned from her job and came to Cape Town. Number five: I'm telling you now, if Martin Fillis got that painting, he wouldn't hesitate for one second. He'd murder her in cold blood, and try to sell the painting. I've looked into that man's eyes, and I tell you now, he will kill.

'But it's number six, Benna, that's a dead give-away. What did Prof Donald Duck do, the moment he realised Alicia Lewis was killed? He did what any normal, innocent, upstanding citizen would do. He called us. And Martin Fillis? Don't tell me he doesn't know about the murder. It's on the TV and radio and the internet, it's on the posters on the lampposts, every newspaper's front page, it was on the front page of *Die Son*, for God's sake. Martin Fillis would read *Die Son* every day, I guarantee it. So that's how we know he's our man, Benna. Come on, we'll have to see Major Mbali because we'll have to be very clever with this psycho. He knows all the tricks of the detective trade, he's had since Monday, plenty of time to cover his tracks, he's probably all lawyered up, and ready with an alibi. We're going to need all the help we can get.'

Despite Griessel's vague unease about Cupido's certainty, they did their homework, discussed their theories and made plans.

In the midst of it all John Cloete phoned and told Benny an article had appeared half an hour ago on the *Guardian* website in the UK, identifying Alicia Lewis as one of the top international experts on the Dutch Masters. The report also asked questions about Lewis's sudden resignation from Restore, and why she travelled to 'dangerous South Africa' for a holiday so soon after her resignation.

'The whole world wants commentary, Benny. Do you have anything?'

'The investigation is at a sensitive stage,' said Griessel.

John Cloete sighed. He had more patience than any man Benny knew.

They called ahead, and drove to Oakglen in Bellville, where Mbali Kaleni had a townhouse. She met them at the gate, wearing mud-caked gardening gloves, a wide-brimmed hat and dark glasses. She smelled of fresh earth and perfume. 'I'm planting a cabbage tree,' she said.

Under normal circumstances Cupido's face would have registered amusement, or irritation, depending on his mood, for Griessel suspected that neither one of them had even envisaged their Zulu commanding officer as a keen – and over-dressed – Saturday-morning gardener. But Vaughn was serious: 'Thanks for seeing us, Major. We've got our guy, but we need your help . . .'

She invited them in. She offered tea, or ice-water with cucumber and lemon; they said thanks, but no thanks.

Cupido told her everything they knew. She listened attentively, and when he had finished, she frowned her famous frown, and asked, 'But why would the Lewis woman choose him, this Fillis person?'

'We wondered the same thing, Major,' said Cupido. 'So we did a test. We Googled the words "Cape Town Private Investigator." His agency, Billy de Palma Private Investigations, was right at the top of the search results, next to a little green logo that says "Ad." Sergeant Davids says it's because Fillis buys those keywords from Google, it's called AdWords. And we had a look at his website too. It's very professional. Big photo of him, he's this big, very handsome guy, that's how he fools a lot of people; he looks trustworthy on a photograph. And the website says he's a former detective inspector with the SAPS. She would have thought he's the perfect guy for the job.'

'I see,' said Kaleni. 'Okay. What have you come to ask me for?'

'He's sly and he's smart, so we want to hit him very hard, Major. We don't want him to know we're coming. We want to bring him in for questioning, but we want to do it in a way that will prevent him from reaching his lawyer. We're going to need back-up, he's a violent man, and he's big. We want to tape the interrogation, we want his lies to be on record from the start. We need search warrants for his office and his home, and a 205 for his cell phone records; we want Philip and his team to do a spiderweb.'

A subpoena according to Article 205 of the Criminal Procedure Act forced cell phone companies to provide the Hawks with complete cell phone records. Captain Philip van Wyk and his team at IMC used special programs to connect all the calls with people – the so-called spiderweb that would show who would have had contact with Fillis.

Kaleni shook her head. 'Captain Cloete called me . . .'

Griessel could see Cupido's shoulders droop. Once the major knew how big and international the media interest was, she would be even more conservative and careful than usual.

'We'll have to be very careful.'

'Yes, Major.'

'You don't have enough for the search warrants.'

They knew that, but they also knew Kaleni – behind that frown was unshakeable loyalty, and a need to support the people around her. Give her something to say 'no' to, and chances were good that she would approve other requests.

'Okay,' said Cupido with mock disappointment.

'But I'll sign the 205 application. And we'll get uniform back-up for the arrest.'

'Thank you, Major.'

They wanted to confront Fillis alone and in public. So Cupido phoned the cell number on the Billy de Palma Private Investigations website, and a man answered, and Cupido recognised the voice. He nodded to Benny, and passed the phone to him. Griessel introduced himself as 'Ben Barnard,' and it was 'Mr de Palma' this and 'Mr de Palma' that, trying also to sound defeated and desperate. He said he wanted to see him urgently, as he was convinced his wife was having an affair, she was going out tonight, and he needed someone to follow her. 'I don't care about the cost, please, can I meet you at the Spur, there's a Spur near your office, the one beside Cavendish Square. I can meet you there, I'll bring you cash, just say how much.'

And then they held their breath as they waited to hear his response.

The cash that Griessel offered was bait, in case Fillis was unwilling to see clients on a Saturday morning. Cash needn't go through the books, he could avoid sales tax and income tax.

They waited, Fillis sighed, and then said, 'Okay. Meet me at half past twelve, I'll be in the smokers' section, wearing a Stormers jersey.'

15

Major Mbali Kaleni rang the SAPS station commander in Claremont. He had to do some juggling because it was mid-Saturday, and most of his men started their shift late afternoon in order to police the evils of Saturday night, and he could only spare them four uniforms.

Griessel and Cupido met them in front of the Rodeo Spur Steak Ranch at 12:33. Griessel went in first to make sure Fillis was there already. At this time on a Saturday the restaurant was a colourful, screaming mass; at least three kiddies' parties were in full swing. He spotted Fillis in the smoking section, in a Stormers rugby jersey as he had promised; the loud, ugly yellow and red of the rugby team's sponsor caught the eye instantly. He turned around and went to fetch Cupido and the uniforms. They marched in through the throng of children. Fillis saw them coming, and from his expression they could tell the moment when he recognised Cupido, and realised this procession was heading towards him. His gaze flicked once towards the door, his only escape route, and that was when they knew they had their man.

Fillis stood up just before they reached his table. His eyes were trained on Cupido, his remark cutting: 'Hello, Vaughn. Still the biggest show-off in the Hawks?'

Griessel saw how big Fillis was, the rugby jersey stretched across his powerful shoulders.

'Martin Reginald Fillis, we have reason to believe you can assist us with information in connection with the murder of Alicia Lewis.'

No reaction.

'We have reason to believe your cell phone contains evidence that will link you to Lewis. Please hand it over.'

Fillis weighed up the uniforms, one of them with a pair of handcuffs in his hand. He looked back at Griessel and Cupido. He said, 'Fuck you, Vaughn.'

'I'll only ask once more for your phone,' said Griessel. 'Or are we looking at an arrest for obstruction?'

Everyone in the restaurant was staring at them. Fillis wavered, and then very slowly reached into his pocket and took out his phone. Benny held out a plastic evidence bag. Fillis dropped his phone into it.

For over half an hour, in the car on the way back to DPCI offices, the detectives were silent. Fillis sat in the back. He only spoke once, when he asked, 'Aren't you Benny Griessel, the alky Hawk?' When there was no response, he lit a cigarette and blew the smoke through the metal grid between them. They knew he was trying to provoke them. They ignored him. Fillis stared out of the window and rubbed his hand over the manicured lines of his goatee beard.

As they got out, Fillis jerked his arm out of Griessel's grip, and Cupido grabbed for his service pistol and cuffs, but Fillis relaxed, and walked between them, down the long, dark, Saturday-silent corridors of the Hawks building, into the interview room. Everyone sat down, everyone knew his place.

'Fuck all of you.' Fillis fired the opening salvo. 'I'm not saying a word without my lawyer.'

They had known he would say just that.

'You can talk to us without your lawyer, or you and your lawyer can talk to the press together,' said Griessel.

Fillis pulled a face and shook his head. '*Jirre*, Vaughn, you're even more stupid than I remember. Was that your best plan? Get me at the Spur with a brilliant con, and then expect me to shit my pants in front of all the little kiddies, and spill the beans? That's the best you Hawks can do? Really?'

'Spill beans about what, Martin?'

'Whatever.'

'Where were you on Monday, Martin?' Griessel asked.

'Ask my lawyer.' Fillis took out his cigarettes and lit one, ignoring the fact that there was no ashtray on the table.

Griessel recognised it as a gesture. A tactic. He ignored it. 'Where were you on Monday, Martin?'

'Ask my lawyer. And go fuck yourself.'

'Let me tell you about our best plan, Martin,' said Griessel. 'Our best plan is to give you the chance to tell us everything. And if you don't want to then we tell the press that you are our number one suspect . . .'

'Billy de Palma. Were you ashamed of your coloured skin, Martin?' Cupido asked.

No response.

'You see, Billy Boy,' said Cupido, 'we know how precious your Billy de Palma brand is. We know about your Google AdWords. We know you invested heavily to be the number one agency popping up in an internet search for a PI agency in the Cape. So, our best plan is to let the newspapers and news sites all run an article or two about you and your agency, and how you might, or might not, be involved in the killing of Alicia Lewis . . .'

'The *Guardian* is writing about it already,' said Griessel.

'That's a big British newspaper,' said Cupido.

'I know what the *Guardian* is.' Angry.

'Then you will know, if prospective clients search for a PI in the Cape on Google next week, what they will find,' said Griessel.

'Or next year,' said Cupido. 'Or in two years' time, that's the trouble with the damn interwebs, Billy Boy, all that info just does not go away. It comes back to haunt you.'

'Then they see your AdWords on the same page as all the links to news reports saying you might, or might not, be a murderer,' said Griessel.

'And we'll tell the media about your past, and they'll put that in too, they love that kind of shit. And they're going to stop calling, Billy Boy, all those clients with errant husbands,' said Cupido.

'All that AdWord money wasted,' said Griessel.

'You'll have to find a new job; your agency will be as dead as a dodo. But horror of horrors, Billy Boy, people will find out you're a fraud. A crook. A two-bit, second-rate, corrupt ex-cop, a beater of prostitutes, a killer of defence-less women.'

And that was their best plan, their gamble: for Fillis to realise he had to give them something, if he wanted to keep his agency's name out of the news. They had no idea whether it would work, but Cupido firmly believed nar-cissists were afraid above all of being humiliated in public.

They kept an eagle eye on him, waited. He sat like the sphinx, staring at the glass of the observation window.

At last: 'I don't know what you're talking about.'

Cupido snorted in amusement. 'We have a 205, we're going to trace all your calls. What will you say then, if we can prove that you had contact with Lewis?'

No answer.

'It's only a question of time before we crack her emails. Help yourself. Tell us where you were on Monday,' Gries-sel asked.

Long silence, before Fillis said, 'I'll have to check my calendar. Pass me my phone.'

Griessel shook his head. 'You know exactly where you were on Monday.'

Fillis crossed his arms across his chest.

'Have it your way,' said Cupido. 'Benna, call the media liaison officer.'

Griessel took out his phone and called John Cloete. The liaison officer answered straight away. Griessel put the phone on speaker: 'John, we're ready to make an arrest, you can let the press know the suspect is Martin Reginald—'

'Okay,' said Fillis, sharply and urgently.

'What's that?' said Cupido.

'Okay, I'll talk.'

'What, without your lawyer?'

Fillis nodded, his back straight, neck rigid, a man battling to retain his dignity.

'Sorry, John, seems I was a little hasty,' said Griessel and cut the call.

16

Fillis swore blind that he had had no contact with Alicia Lewis, not on Sunday and not on Monday. He had never in his life met her in person. The last he had heard from her was more than two months ago.

'So, we'll plot your phone, and it will show us that you were nowhere near her on Monday?'

'I don't know where she was on Monday.'

'Start at the beginning,' said Griessel. 'When did she contact you?'

Fillis told his story with shifty eyes and aggressive, staccato sentences. He said he received an email from her out of the blue the previous November. Initially she simply asked him to confirm that one of his specialities was tracing people, as his website promised. He assured her that it was. In the next email she asked if he would be prepared to help locate a missing object, which might be in the possession of one of nine different people. He replied to her that his skills included that service. Alicia Lewis phoned him from London the next day, and spoke to him in person, an explorative discussion about his background and rates; he reckoned it was to probe him. Apparently she was satisfied, as she sent him a contract with an extended confidentiality clause. He signed it and returned it, and then received the nine names.

'By then you knew who she was,' said Cupido.

'How would I know, Vaughn?' Angered by the suggestion.

'Because I know you, Billy Boy. You would have Googled her long before. You would know that this aunty works with heavy-duty paintings; if she was looking for something, it meant big bucks. So you started scheming . . .'

Fillis swore at Cupido, and Cupido snorted, and they argued back and forth about the fairness of Cupido's statement, until Griessel said, 'So you tracked the people down?'

'Of course I tracked them down. I'm the best PI in the land.'

'Never believe your own press, Billy Boy. And who had the painting?'

'The farmer in Villiersdorp.'

Their ears pricked up, hearts racing, but they were too experienced to let Fillis see how the news excited them.

'What farmer in Villiersdorp?'

'Vermeulen. Willem Vermeulen. Senior.'

'How do you know that, Billy Boy? How do you know?'

'I asked him. And he said, *ja*, he'd seen the painting, so I asked where, and he said it was none of my business.'

'So how could he see what painting you were looking for?'

'I showed him a photo.'

'What photo?'

'The one that Lewis sent me.'

'A photo?'

'Are you deaf?'

'Why didn't you tell us she sent you a photo?'

'You didn't give me the chance,' he replied with a grin over his small victory.

'If you want to play games, Billy Boy, we can also play games. Benna, I told you he's a piece of shit. Let's call the media, and be done with it. He's going to try and lead us round the bush all the time . . .'

'It was just a piece of the painting,' said Fillis irritably. 'First she sent the nine names. I found eight of them. One woman is dead, August last year in Pretoria, but that didn't matter in the end. I sent her the eight addresses. Then she sent the photo of the painting by email. Just a section of the whole painting, it turns out. Of a woman's face. A woman in a cape.'

'A cape? What do you mean? Like in Cape Town?'

'No, a cape, like in Superman.'

Griessel asked where the photograph was. Fillis replied that it was in an email on his phone. Griessel took the private detective's phone out of his pocket, and navigated by Fillis's instructions to the Gmail application, the correct folder and the right email. They looked at the photo of a section of a painting, showing the head and shoulders of a woman. She was looking straight at them with dark brown eyes, not smiling, but her mouth seemed ready to do so. There was a softness in her gaze, a tenderness, knowledge. They couldn't stop staring at her, the beautiful red lips, the nose, not small, but right for this face, the smooth pale white skin, light brown hair tied back from her face. A very attractive woman.

But the object that caused Benny Griessel to blurt out the words was the cape over her shoulders. It seemed from this piece of the painting to be the only garment she was wearing. But it was the colour that inspired him.

'The woman in blue,' he said.

'Exactly,' said Cupido.

'What?' asked Fillis.

Cupido's phone began to ring. 'None of your business, Billy Boy,' he said, taking the phone out of his pocket. He recognised the number, answered it, listened, and said, 'Okay, okay. What road is it? Okay, thank you very much, please phone PCSI.' He ended the call and told Griessel. 'Grabouw station found her car. The rental. On the mountain the other side of Grabouw, on the way to Villiersdorp. Smells awfully of Jik. Now we have you, Billy Boy. Your plan has come to naught . . .'

They phoned Major Mbali Kaleni and said they had enough for the search warrants for Fillis's office and home. They asked for reinforcements. Specifically asked for Captains 'Mooiwillem' Liebenberg and Frankie Fillander to continue questioning Martin Fillis. Those two were also on duty this weekend and were always willing, and they knew Fillis-the-narcissist would be endlessly irritated for his time to be wasted by a man more handsome than he was. Liebenberg was called the George Clooney of the Hawks and 'Uncle' Frank Fillander had more experience and people-sense than anyone on the Serious and Violent Crimes unit.

It took nearly an hour to bring Liebenberg and Fillander up to date on the case. They also asked their two colleagues to draw out the interrogation of Fillis as long as possible, while they drove out to a farm in the Villiersdorp district.

Cupido and Griessel took the N2 over Sir Lowry's Pass, and drove through Grabouw. They phoned Jimmy, the long skinny PCSI man, for directions to the location of Alicia Lewis's hired Toyota.

'Take the R321 out of Grabouw, and drive towards Theewaterskloof Dam, about twelve kilometres. The gate is on the right going up the mountain. You'll see a SAPS van and two constables.'

They had no eyes for the breathtaking natural beauty, the blue farm dams, the dark green pine forests and grey rock formations in the rugged mountains. They discussed and reconsidered the case, alert for the police van, found it, and turned off the main road. It was a farm gate, with a tiny signboard, half obscured by vegetation, that read *Groenlandberg Nature Reserve. No entry.*

The constables said they responded when a warden from the reserve called the charge office at Grabouw when he found the Toyota abandoned there.

'Was this gate locked?' Griessel asked.

'No, Captain, it isn't locked.'

'Are Forensics here yet?'

'Yes, Captain, just a hundred metres further on.'

They walked. It was a rough jeep track, winding up the mountain. They spotted the white Forensics minibus first, then Thick and Thin busy with Alicia Lewis's grey rented Toyota. The vehicle's doors, boot and bonnet were open. Thick and Thin saw the detectives and came to them. They were full of their usual wisecracks, complaining that they were going to miss the Stormers' rugby match against the Free State Cheetahs.

Arnold, the short fat one, explained that the Toyota had been wiped clean of fingerprints from top to bottom, and the inside was so badly washed with bleach that it had chewed holes in the carpets and seat covers. He couldn't have done a more thorough job of removing all forensic traces.

'My point exactly,' said Cupido. 'It's someone who knows exactly what to do.'

The name of the farm was Eden. The beautiful homestead was situated high up in the mountains east of the town; the view over the Theewaterskloof Dam was spectacular.

They parked in front of the door, and three large dogs ran barking from the veranda and escorted them with wagging tails to the wide-open front door. They rang the bell, hearing the sound of rugby commentary from deep within the house. At last, a heavy tread on the wooden floorboards, and a man appeared in the hallway – a large man, in his forties, with thick forearms and massive hands.

'Good afternoon,' he said. 'Can I help you?'

'We're from the police. The Hawks. We're here about the painting,' said Griessel.

The man stood still in his dark tracksuit and slippers. He stared at them without expression. Then he sighed, as if in relief. He put out a large hand. 'Junior Vermeulen.'

They shook hands, introduced themselves. Griessel said, 'We're actually looking for Willem Vermeulen Senior.'

'That's my father. But no, you're looking for me. If it's about the painting, you're looking for me.'

He invited them in, called deeper into the house. 'We've got people, *vrou*, turn off that TV, WP are going to lose this match anyway.' He led them down the passage, lined with ceiling-high bookshelves packed with books, and invited them to sit in the formal sitting room, on big old classic chairs. The sound of the TV stopped, lighter footsteps approached. His wife was plump and pretty, with deep dimples when she smiled. She touched a hand to her hair, saying, 'Excuse me, we weren't expecting people. I'm Minnie.'

'They're here about the painting,' said her husband.

'About time,' she said. 'Can I offer you something to drink?'

It took a while as each one expressed their preferences of what was on offer. Then the three men sat down again, and Junior Vermeulen asked, 'Any news?'

The question took them by surprise. Cupido asked, 'What do you mean?'

'Well, if you're here, you must have some news, I assume?'

'News about what, Mr Vermeulen?'

'About the painting. That is why you're here?'

'We are here about Alicia Lewis.'

'Oh?'

'You know Alicia Lewis?'

'Yes, yes, she was here on Monday,' he said somewhat testily. 'What's the problem with her?'

The detectives looked at each other, and then back at him. 'She's dead, Mr Vermeulen,' Griessel said.

'Oh, *hell*,' said the farmer. 'How?'

'Haven't you seen the news, Mr Vermeulen?'

'No, I don't watch the news any more. It's the same bad news every day. How did she die?'

'She was murdered on Monday . . .'

'Oh, *hell*!' Vermeulen stood up abruptly, startling the detectives so that they instinctively reached for their service pistols. He turned his back on them and stopped in the doorway and shouted to the kitchen: '*Vrou*, they say the Lewis woman is dead. On Monday, too. Murdered.'

'No!' Minnie Vermeulen cried out, and her footsteps hurried back towards them. She asked how and where Alicia Lewis was murdered, her voice filled with consternation and confusion. Her husband tried to console her, but she kept insisting, tearfully, 'The poor woman, it's my fault, it's all my fault.'

'No, no, it isn't,' her husband comforted her, and eventually Griessel told them both: 'Please come and sit down.'

Vermeulen said, '*Vrou*, I think it's best the truth comes out now.'

'Yes,' she said quietly.

'Will you come with us, please,' he said.

'Where to?'

'I want to show you the painting.'

17

12 October

They were a few hundred paces behind him, the four.
Like demons, they didn't tire. He walked into Delft, after
ten, not sure what the time was. He wanted to follow the
Oude Langendijk to the Groot Markt; perhaps he could
lose them there if his legs and breath held out. He couldn't
go on, it was now or never, they were too close, the four
of them, and they never seemed to tire. For the first time
panic overwhelmed him, his breath came fast and ragged,
as he imagined the daggers stabbing him, how his blood

would spatter and spray like a slaughtered sheep. He choked back the urge to scream out loud, broke into a run, no, he must not, it was too early, he must conserve his strength, wait for the crowds at the Groot Markt. He still had a tiny lead, but fear overwhelmed him, dulled his senses. He looked over his shoulder: they were running too, a blade glinted in the bright sun. 'Lord, help me!' He didn't know if it was a silent thought, or screamed from his lips. This was how it was going to end, in Delft, in Doelen Street in Delft, a place to which he had no connection, no kin; he would die as a stranger, they would bury him in an unmarked grave somewhere, no one would ever know about him . . .

The invisible hand lifted him up. He saw his feet leave the ground, and in the moment he thought, I'm dead, I'm flying! The hand threw him with incredible force against the wall of the house, a thunderclap that shot searing pain through his ears. He cried again to heaven, heard his ribs break, that was all he could hear, his own bones cracking, all dark, all dark. He felt the agony, his chest, his head, his ears.

Something lay on top of him, heavy; he opened his eyes in terror, only his right hand could move. He wiped his eyes, there was blood on his hand. Had they got him?

The wall, it was the wall that was pressing down on him; he shifted, such agony, but he could move, he could push the broken fragments of the wall off him. But why was he deaf? He surged up, he had to see where they were. Pain shot through his side, his ribs.

He saw devastation, houses on fire, the four who had been pursuing him were gone, completely gone, as if the Higher Hand had raptured them.

Then he spotted the blue, between the dark ashen greys of the beams and stone and rubble and soot. The bright, bright splash of blue.

He stumbled towards it, a patch of colour, a fragment of life.

Gingerly he picked it up, saw the figure of the woman. And gasped.

18

It took their breath away.

Against a bleached white background with a texture so real you could feel it, the woman stood – the same woman, exactly the same as the one in Fillis's photo. But now you could see her from head to toe. Beneath the blue cloak she was completely naked. Her feet rested in the water of a stream or fountain or bath, and she held the cape closed with both hands to cover her breasts and her womanhood. Her belly, round as if with child, strong legs visible from high above the knees. And that face, those eyes, full of secrets and compassion.

All that bathed in beautiful, magical light.

The painting hung in the Vermeulen's large walk-in gun safe, in the cellar under the house. The detectives stared at the painting; the farmer and his wife looked at them.

'So beautiful, and now a woman is dead . . .' said Minnie.

'That's nothing to do with us, *vrou.*'

'But, Junior . . .'

Benny and Vaughn heard, but couldn't stop staring at the painting.

'We think she is Hendrickje Stoffels,' said Minnie.

'Okay,' said Cupido, the enchantment of the woman and the painting still holding him in its grip.

'What?' asked Griessel.

'Rembrandt's mistress,' said Minnie. 'Rembrandt often painted her, that's how we know what she looked like. But this is the only painting showing her pregnant. That was in 1654, shortly before Fabritius died. There was a bit of a scandal about her . . .'

'Now I'm confused,' said Cupido.

'Me too,' said Griessel.

'She and Fabritius have that effect on people,' said Minnie. 'Look here, see this burn mark?'

They looked. On the left edge of the painting a small section was missing, and the edges were burned black.

They nodded.

'Come on, let's have a cup of coffee, and I'll tell you everything.'

She told the tale with dignity, the farmer's wife with the dimples in her cheeks. With the help of her husband. She said this was the version she believed, though there was little concrete proof of the story.

She said that Carel Fabritius's real name was Carel Pietersz. But that was not important. Fabritius was a pupil of the famous Rembrandt van Rijn. Fifteen years after he had studied under him, in the summer of 1654, Fabritius visited his old teacher in Amsterdam, and saw that Rembrandt's mistress and former housekeeper was pregnant with their first child. Back in Delft, Fabritius completed the painting of Hendrickje, probably as a gift for Rembrandt. He must have finished it before October 1654.

At half past ten on the morning of 12 October 1654 the manager of the Kruithuis, the powder magazine where they stored the town's gunpowder, entered the building with a lantern. Nobody will ever know precisely what happened, but the explosion, known as the Delfse Donderslag, the Delft Thunderclap, flattened more than a quarter of the city. It was heard a hundred and fifty kilometres away.

Carel Fabritius, the genial painter with a big career ahead of him, was at home when the Kruithuis exploded. He died instantly, and almost all the paintings that he had been working on at the time were destroyed.

'I think that little burned spot on the edge of the painting happened at the Delfse Donderslag,' said Minnie Vermeulen. 'And I think someone picked it up there and I think that man was a Van Schoorl. But let me jump ahead three hundred and fifty years or so, so you can understand why I think that.'

The painting, she said, which was done on wood, incidentally, had been in her husband's family for many generations. When she married Junior, she saw it hanging in the master bedroom in the farmhouse, when the farm still belonged to her father-in-law, Willem Vermeulen Senior.

It enchanted everyone who saw it, but few were given the privilege. Senior was a staunch churchman, and the near-nakedness of the woman was not something he liked to flaunt.

When Junior took over the farming, she asked if the painting could stay in the bedroom. 'Very well,' her father-in-law said. 'But you're not to show it off. Promise me.'

She promised.

Minnie Vermeulen explained that she was a reader. From a young age. She read anything, but she was always behind with her reading, because there are so many good books, and so little time. It was only last year in April that she got round to reading Donna Tartt's book, *The Goldfinch*.

'Wait a minute,' said Cupido.

'That's what the prof talked about,' said Griessel.

'That's right,' said Cupido. 'What's with the Tartt woman?'

The farmer's wife said Donna Tartt was an American author who wrote a very popular novel called *The Goldfinch*, about a painting of a goldfinch by the same Fabritius. The real goldfinch painting is on display in the Mauritshuis in The Hague in the Netherlands. But all that was not important. What was important, was that the Tartt book made Minnie Vermeulen get up from her reading chair out on the back veranda, and go to the painting in the bedroom.

She knew she had seen the name Fabritius before, and she was sure it was on the bottom of the picture that hung in front of their bed.

And she saw that it was – in the same Roman letters and handwriting, and the same year as *The Goldfinch* painting.

'I couldn't believe it. I didn't want to believe it. I rubbed my fingertips over the oil paint to make sure it was genuine. I went to find Junior and asked him how old the painting was. I talked to my father-in-law, read everything about Fabritius that I could find, and then I started scratching around in the history in the archives to try and find out if it was genuine. I knew, if it was really a Fabritius, it would be worth a lot of money.

'I didn't have proof for everything, but I believe a man by the name of Van Schoorl picked up the painting near Fabritius's house the day the Kruithuis exploded in Delft. And I think he boarded a ship by the name of *Arnhem* two weeks later and sailed to the Cape to work for the Dutch East India Company. And I think his son sold the painting twenty years later to one of Junior's forefathers, a Van Reenen.'

She said there was really only one way to be completely sure that it was genuine, and that was to share the painting with experts. But they weren't ready for that, because her father-in-law lived close by in town, and she had promised not to show the painting to anyone.

So she searched on the internet, and came across the website of a company called Restore, and their expert on the Dutch painters of that time, Alicia Lewis.

'So I took a photo of the painting and sent it to Alicia Lewis—'

'Without saying a word to me,' Junior interrupted.

'That's true, I can't deny it. I just wanted to hear first if there was anything in it, you understand? Anyway, I sent the photo to the woman and asked her if she thought it might be a genuine Fabritius. Within the day I had an email reply, and she said it might be, and could she phone me, please. And I thought, oh, no, goodness, what if she starts telling the world there's a Fabritius here. Pa Senior will murder me, and I said, no, I don't have a phone, she can just email me. Then, a few days later, she sent me a bunch of photos of Rembrandt's paintings of Hendrickje Stoffels, and she said, I must take a good look, is that not the same woman? I compared them, and I could see the likeness, the chances were good it was the same woman. So I wrote back to her, yes, I do think it is the same woman, and her next email was this awfully long one saying she was sending me a contract, she would like to represent me, and I owe it to the world to reveal and display the painting, and do I realise, if it is genuine, it was worth over a billion rand. That gave me an enormous fright. Enormous.'

That was when she took the whole story to her husband. Junior asked her what the Lewis woman knew about them. She said nothing, except her email address – minnie43@mweb.co.za.

'Just leave it then, *vrou*,' said Junior. 'Pa will disown us, and we don't need the money, and we don't need the fuss. And it will cause a major drama, this thing . . .'

The farmer leaned forward now, and said, '*Ja*, that didn't help, because last November, that detective arrived here at the farm with a little picture on his phone, and I said no, Pa lives in town, and he asked, do you know this painting?'

'It's the same photo that I sent to Alicia Lewis,' said Minnie. 'But his was just cut much smaller, so you could only see Hendrickje's face and a piece of the cloak.'

'Martin Fillis?' asked Cupido. 'Was that the detective's name?'

'No, it wasn't . . .'

'Billy de Palma.'

'That's it. De Palma. And idiot that I am,' said Junior, 'I'm such a bad liar that I long ago stopped trying. I told him, yes, I've seen the painting. And he asked, where? And I started to understand and I said, why do you want to know? And he hummed and hah-ed, but he didn't want to say, and I said, then we have nothing to talk about. And he left again.'

'Junior came to tell me and I said, Junior, let's put it in the safe, in case someone tries to steal our Fabritius. So we did. And I took my photo, and had it enlarged and framed it, and we put that there in front of the bed, so that I can still see Hendrickje, because by now we are best friends . . .

'We'd barely hung it up, one Sunday, when we came out of church after the *nagmaal* service in town, and when I switched my phone back on, the security people had left a message to say the house alarm had gone off and we must come. The only thing that was stolen out of that whole house was the photo of the Fabritius on our bedroom wall, my pearls that were in the little box on my dressing table, under the picture, and two bottles of preserved peaches from the kitchen.'

'And then?'

'I installed a bigger, thicker door on the strongroom.'

19

'I thought you said you'd found the stolen goods,' said Willem Vermeulen Junior. 'That's why I asked you if you had any news, about the painting, earlier. When we reported the theft to the local police, we said it was a picture of a woman in a blue cloak. In any case, we thought, that would be the last we would hear about it. Until Monday.'

'There was a knock on the door, around half past eleven. Junior was in the vineyards, I was in the kitchen baking Hertzog cookies, and I went to see. There was a woman there, smartly dressed, and she said, "Good morning, I'm looking for Willem Vermeulen," and I said, I'm Minnie Vermeulen, pleased to meet you, and she gave me a look, and said, "Minnie. Of course. Minnie. We've spoken before. Via email. My name is Alicia Lewis."'

'And then?'

'I invited her in, and sent someone to fetch Willem from the vineyards, because I was scared now, I had brought all this on myself, I was the one who sent the photo and the email and now here she was. She asked straight away to see the Fabritius, and I said, "No, there's bad news, just wait for my husband to come," and when he came in, I told him in Afrikaans that he must play along with my lie. We told her the painting was stolen, and she could check with the police, we had reported the theft.'

'And then?'

'She wouldn't believe us. I showed her the place where it used to hang in the bedroom. She cried then, right there in our room. I had to comfort her, and I felt so awfully bad, she was crying because I lied to her, but we persisted with it. She had lunch with us, and she asked how big and how beautiful the painting was, and then she left.'

'At what time?'

'Probably . . . It was late, she stayed a long time, like she didn't want to leave. Must have been about half past three?'

Junior agreed.

'When did she die?' Minnie Vermeulen asked.

'Shortly after,' said Griessel.

'Ay, *Heretjie*,' said Minnie, and she began to sob again.

The sun was setting when they drove back to Bellville. Griessel had the wheel; he phoned Mooiwillem Liebenberg to hear how he was getting on with Martin Fillis.

'He's still sitting here. Looks like his alibi for Monday is watertight. Uncle Frankie is still verifying some details, but Fillis was at his office. A check on his cell phone confirms that's true, there's a camera at his building's reception that shows him entering, and at least one of his clients says they had a meeting with him around three o'clock.'

'Damn . . . What about a contract killing, Willem?'

'His phone records for the last month show nothing suspicious, Vaughn. Only if you go further back . . .'

'Yes?'

'Philip and his team found one flag on the system: there was a flurry of calls between Fillis and a man by the name of Rudewaan Ismail. More than thirty-four calls, back and forth, over a few weeks. Now, Ismail has an impressive record. He's been to jail seven times for housebreaking, he's a pro—'

'When, Willem? When did Fillis have contact with Ismail?'

'Let me see . . .'

'November? December?'

'That's right, early December. They talked a few times a day, up till the fourteenth.'

'Is there a last known address for Ismail?' Cupido asked.

'Yes, Mitchells Plain . . .'

'Ask them to bring him in, Willem. For the theft of a painting on a farm outside Villiersdorp . . .'

Griessel and Cupido went to join Uncle Frank Fillander and Mooiwillem Liebenberg who were still interrogating Fillis. Fillis wasn't sitting down any more, he was pacing up and down the room and cursing them, saying he was going to sue the Hawks and the entire SAPS. The floor was littered with cigarette butts and the place reeked of old smoke.

'Go ahead,' said Cupido. 'But let me tell you something, Billy Boy. We're going to nail you. Your pal Rudewaan Ismail is on his way to pay us a visit. And he's going to make a deal with us, I can guarantee it.'

'Fuck you, Vaughn.' But now he looked anxious. 'I want food and water and cigarettes, I'm not talking to you any more.'

They walked out. Fillis swore after them.

They went to Cupido's office to call the Villiersdorp police station. They needed the dossiers of the break-ins.

Rudewaan Ismail was forty-one years old, slim as a reed, with a pencil moustache and a very humble and submissive manner. They sat with him in Cupido's office. 'No, sieurs,' he said, using the old-fashioned deferential address, 'the criminal record, the guilty verdicts, it was all a misunderstanding, the stuff was planted on me, I'm not the kind that steals.'

'All seven times, brother?' Cupido asked.

'Hard to believe, I know, but it's true, sieurs.'

'Sieurs. That's old school, my bru'.'

'That's the way I am.'

'Rudewaan, you know Martin Fillis . . .'

'I couldn't really say, sieur . . .'

'No, we know that you know him. We have records of your many phone calls in December and we have Fillis himself over there in the interrogation room, and he's singing like a canary. He says it's you who did the burglaries, not him. He just whispered in your ear . . .'

'No, sieur, that doesn't ring a bell.' But his eyes had suddenly become restless.

'The thing is, Rudewaan, he wants to nail you for the crime. He wants to walk out of here free as a bird, and you're going back to the *tjoekie*. That's not right.'

'But it's just his word against mine, sieur . . .'

'No, it's not,' Griessel lied. 'We know you were wearing gloves during the burglaries, Rudewaan. But our forensic guys found some of your hair at the scene. Hair always falls out, and now we're going to test that hair for DNA, and then we can place you at the scene. You will go back to jail.'

'Ay, sieur . . .'

'Here's the deal, Rudewaan,' said Cupido. 'We're not after you; we want that snake, Fillis. I swear to you, tonight you'll walk away a free man if you tell the truth. I'm your get-out-of-jail-free card . . .'

'Ay, sieur . . .'

'Last chance, Rudewaan . . .'

'The judge is going to put you away for a looong time,' said Griessel.

'Will you put the deal in writing for me, sieur?'

'You're old school, but you're not stupid, hey, bru'.'

A tiny, nervous smile behind the pencil moustache. 'No, sieur, I'm not stupid.'

Rudewaan Ismail told them that Martin Fillis had caught him for housebreaking eight years ago, when Fillis was still a detective at Caledon Square. 'But he didn't arrest me; he said from then on he wanted five hundred rand a month protection money.' Ismail paid it, until one night in Durbanville he was caught red-handed and sent to jail.

'And then, end of last year, Fillis turned up, first time in I don't know how many years that I saw him, and he said he would give me ten thousand to steal a painting from a farm for him. There by Villiersdorp.'

'What painting?'

'*Die vrou met die blou.*'

'What?'

'*Vrou met die blou.* The lady in blue. That's what Fillis called it. He showed me a little photo, and said, bring me *die vrou met die blou.*'

The detectives exchanged a significant look.

'Okay, carry on.'

'So I went to chat with the people who work on the farm, and I saw that, no, Sunday during church was the best time. That's when I broke in, and there in the bedroom I saw the lady in blue, the same one as in the photo, and I stole her. I took it to Fillis, but he said, no, you imbecile, this isn't a painting, any idiot can see it's a photograph. So I said, but it's the only woman in blue in the whole house, and I wanted my money. He said, then the painting must be in the old man's house, and I asked what old man, and he said, never mind, here's the address. So I went and stole all the paintings at that house. But there wasn't a woman in blue among them. So he hasn't paid me a cent. That's why I don't really mind ratting on the bastard.'

They arrested Martin Fillis of Billy de Palma Private Investigations on charges of accessory to burglary, conspiracy and dealing in stolen goods. They sat down with Mooiwillem Liebenberg and Frankie Fillander, and questioned Fillis relentlessly, till well after midnight, about his activities on Monday. They studied his phone records and questioned his alibis, but they got nothing but curses and his insistence on calling his lawyer.

They locked Fillis in the cells at Bellville Police Station for the night, and drove home after one in the morning.

Vaughn Cupido was still certain that Fillis had something to do with the death of Alicia Lewis. He just didn't know where they would find any evidence.

Benny Griessel didn't share his colleague's suspicions. His heart was in his boots. He knew they didn't have a single true suspect.

20

Griessel was up again by seven, and he and Alexa sat at
their big kitchen table drinking their morning coffee. He
was totally preoccupied with the painting and the investigation, telling her about the strange spellbinding attrac-
tion of the Fabritius portrait and its incredible journey,
from an explosion in a town in the Netherlands three
hundred and sixty years ago, to the walk-in strongroom
of a farmhouse in Villiersdorp on the southern tip of
Africa. A painting that might be worth a billion rand, but
to the owners the dignity and sense of propriety of an

aged, retired farmer were more important than the money and probable fame.

Alexa listened attentively, as always. Her face radiated admiration for him, and her fingers empathetically touched his hand every now and then. It was moments like these that convinced him that marrying her was the right thing to do. Moments when she made him feel worthy and useful and important and appreciated. And loved.

How did you explain that to Cupido?

She said she was going to cook him a nice cheese and mushroom omelette. He said he must get back to the office in a hurry, he would just eat Weet-Bix.

'Go and shower, and when you come back your omelette will be ready.'

'Thank you, Alexa.' With a silent prayer that the omelette would at least be reasonably edible.

While he was in the shower he heard her come into the bathroom: 'Your telephone keeps ringing.'

He slid the shower door open, holding his towel in one hand.

'Who is it?'

'I don't know, it's just a number.'

He looked at it. *Two missed calls.*

'Thanks, Alexa,' he said, drying his hands, and took the phone from her. Standing there in his birthday suit, he called the number back.

A voice answered straight away. 'Hello, this is Willie.'

'My name is Benny Griessel. You called me.'

'Oh, yes, you're the captain of the Hawks? The one who's investigating the Bleached Body case?'

An excited male voice.

'That's right.'

'Man, I think I've got a photo of the murderer.'

Griessel's heart sank. With every investigation you got your jokers and your crazies, the smart alecks, the obsessive and the lonely, phoning in with their suggestions and solutions, criticisms and theories.

'Where did you get my number?'

'Yes, that was quite a thing. From your forensic chaps. I talked to the police in Grabouw first, who gave me the number of the forensic people, and then the Arnold guy said I should talk to you.'

'And the photo?' He was sure now it was one of Arnold's jokes.

'I'm with the Cape Leopard Trust. I'm actually based in Betty's Bay, but we have nearly fifty cameras, from the Groot Winterhoek Mountains at Porterville, to the Kogelberg here. We set up the cameras to photograph the leopards. When they walk between the sensor and the camera, it interrupts the beam and it takes a photo. We're researching their numbers and movements.'

'Okay,' said Griessel, with the first inkling that this might not be a joke after all.

'After the rain we battled a bit, yesterday, with so much mud on the mountain tracks, and I was running late. By the time I got to the Groenland Mountain cameras it was already dark, so I just changed the memory card in the camera and came home. When I checked the photos this morning there was a leopard, a Toyota, a Volkswagen, and then a bunch of policemen, and a minibus with SAPS Provincial Crime Scene Investigation Unit on the side. I phoned the police in Grabouw, and they told me they found the car there yesterday. Of the Bleached Body woman.'

'That's right.'

'Well, I've got a photo of the man who drove the car in there. Date stamp on the photo says Monday night, just after eleven.'

Griessel asked where the man on the phone was speaking from, and he said he was at his house in Betty's Bay, but he would bring the original memory card with the photos on it to them, he didn't want it to 'disappear or something.'

Benny thanked him, hurriedly pulling on some clothes while explaining to Alexa he wasn't going to have time to eat an omelette after all. She fetched him some of the rusks she always bought from Woolworths Food, put them in a plastic bag, and then in his jacket pocket, while he phoned Vaughn Cupido. His colleague said, 'We've got him, Benna, we're going to nail that lowlife Fillis today, I'm telling you now.'

In the car he munched on the dry but delicious muesli rusks, not waiting for coffee to dunk them in. He was first to arrive at work: Cupido turned up ten minutes later and they waited impatiently outside on the steps of the DPCI building for Willie Bruwer, leopard researcher.

'You should have told the guy to email the photos,' said Cupido.

'He was so keen to bring them to us,' said Griessel. 'I think he wants to be a small part of this.'

'His moment of glory . . .'

They waited nearly a quarter of an hour, until a Land-cruiser turned the corner of Voortrekker Street with squealing tyres, made a wide U-turn, and stopped in front of them. Bruwer was young; Griessel guessed he wasn't much past twenty-four. He was wearing the khaki and green clothes of a nature conservation officer. He gave a wave of the hand, got out, slamming the door of the vehicle shut, and strode towards them with a black carrying case in his hand.

He introduced himself, shook hands with them both. Cupido invited him in, and in the deserted reception area of the Hawks, at the desk where Mavis sat on weekdays, Bruwer fired up his laptop, pushed in the memory card, and accessed the photographs. First the female leopard, and then the white Toyota.

The face of the driver wasn't clear, but there was more than enough detail to identify him.

'Well, you could blow me over with a bloody feather,' said Vaughn Cupido. 'I don't believe it.'

They stopped at the entry room of the Schonenberg Retirement Village at 10:24. Both men got out and presented their SAPS ID cards to the guard at the gate. 'We're here to see Prof Marius Wilke. Open the gate and don't tell him we're coming.'

'The prof has gone to church,' the guard said.

That deflated them. They had been all fired up and ready to confront him.

'Is this the only gate?'

'Yes.'

'What time will he be back?'

'About half past eleven, if they don't go out to eat. Some Sundays they eat here at Waterstone's.'

'They?'

'Him and the Hulk.'

'Who's the Hulk?'

'Prof's driver. He doesn't drive himself any more.' Then: 'Bertie,' with a certain tone, and a fingertip tapped on the temple. 'A little bit soft up here.'

They gave the guard precise instructions, then they drove in, to Marius Wilke's house.

'I'm an idiot,' said Griessel while they sat watching from the street.

'Why, Benna?'

'Wilke told me he doesn't drive any more. I should have asked him how he got to the hotel, for his breakfast with Lewis.'

'No, Benna, there's lots of ways, these days. Uber, taxis, the train . . .'

Griessel shook his head. 'No, I don't see him in one of those.'

'Well then, we were both idiots.'

At 11:37 the guard phoned. 'They've just gone through.'

Less than a minute later they saw the Volkswagen Caddy bus turn the corner. They got out and waited for the vehicle. It stopped in the middle of the road, fifty metres from them. They could see the professor's snow-white head, and behind the wheel, a bulky shape.

The Caddy idled, its doors still closed. They walked closer, and could see Wilke talking and gesticulating, his sturdy companion just sitting and listening to him. Cupido drew his service pistol, held it against his side. Griessel did the same. They walked faster.

The door opened on the passenger side. Wilke got out. 'Old Vaughn . . .' But this time the smile was forced.

Cupido raised his pistol and aimed it at the big man behind the steering wheel. 'Tell him to switch off, Prof. Now!'

Wilke spoke into the vehicle; they couldn't hear what he said. Without a word, both of them broke into a run. Griessel was closest to the driver; he saw that the man's eyes were wild, flickering between them and the professor. 'Turn off the vehicle, or I'll shoot,' Griessel shouted, seeing the fear in the big man's eyes, knowing he was going to do something.

'Bertie, do as they say!' Marius Wilke's shrill duck-voice cut through everything, a sharp command.

Bertie switched off the Caddy, and slowly raised his hands.

In the Somerset West police station they showed the photo to Prof Marius Wilke, the one where he sat behind the wheel of Alicia Lewis's rented Toyota. He looked at it, and let out a long deep sigh. 'It was an accident. I swear to you, it was an accident. She fell. There at the bridge over the Theewaterskloof Dam. It was just an accident. But I knew nobody would believe us. I knew.'

They recorded him with a video camera and with their phones. He said, 'Old Benny, I didn't tell you the whole truth.'

But at least he had shared some of the truth with them: he had done the research on the painting, he had found the reference to the painting by Thibault, that wonderful, honest, clever, versatile man. The artwork was part of the Cape, part of the tapestry of history that was woven into this land. He had researched the family tree of Gysbert van Reenen for Alicia Lewis. All the way back to the one who had bought the painting, right down to Willem Vermeulen Junior. Cape people. South Africans. Part of *this* region. This country. Which meant it was South African: the Fabritius painting was part of the very marrow and bone of the Cape. And South Africa.

And they had to understand, someone had to preserve the heritage. But people didn't care any more, nobody cared about history and culture, not even about *Die Taal*, the Afrikaans language; everyone was just chasing after money and fame now. He had seen, through his entire life, how the country's history and its precious historical artefacts were neglected and defaced, how Afrikaans was attacked and broken down. Now, in the last year or two, the artworks and statues on campuses were being burned and broken in the name of decolonisation and Rhodes Must Fall and other senseless campaigns. Surely we couldn't deny our own history? Or change it? Couldn't people understand that we had to know where we came from to know who we were, and where we were heading?

Marius Wilke kept on talking in that vein, a constant stream of words and passion and pleading in his shrill voice. He told them that he had tried to track down the nine people himself, but progress had been too slow.

Then he heard from Alicia Lewis again, recently. And he said, she was coming to the Cape, and he had once promised her a book. That's when he knew she had found the painting. And so he saw his chance: he went and had breakfast with her and took her his best book, so that hopefully she could understand the Cape history and appreciate it a little. So that she could look kindly on his earnest plea. At the hotel, that morning, he begged her: don't allow greed to rule. Don't take the painting out of the country. Let it stay here. Make it known, but help to keep it here.

But she laughed at him, and she took his book and left.

21

So he got into the car with Bertie and told him they were going to wait there outside the hotel, watch for her to come out and then follow her.

Lewis drove to Franschhoek. Over the Franschhoek Pass, to Theewaterskloof. To Villiersdorp. Through to the other side, to the farm, Eden, owned by Willem and Minnie Vermeulen.

That was one of the names on the list that he had sent to Lewis. Willem Vermeulen.

Then he knew that was where the painting was. She had come to get it.

He and Bertie waited, and when Lewis left late in the afternoon, they wanted to see what the painting looked like. Yes, he wanted to see it very badly. It was probably the only time in his life that he would have that privilege, he was an old man already. After all, he had researched and traced it, he had earned the right.

Yes, he wanted to see the painting, and he wanted one last chance to try and persuade her not to take it out of the country. He believed he could reason with her: his intellect and logic, his clarity of reason had often swayed people. And after all, she was an intelligent woman.

Griessel and Cupido had heard many confessions in their lives. Marius Wilke's voice kept rising in tone, as his emotions were heightened. His slight frame jerked and twisted with every revelation, the face, eyes, his whole body combined in a frenzied, frenetic attempt to persuade them that this was the truth.

He had instructed Bertie to overtake her Toyota, and force her to pull over.

On the bridge across the dam he managed it, she was forced to slow and stop at the side of the road. Alicia Lewis was furious, she had jumped out of her car, shouting, 'How dare you, how dare you!' at him. He tried to calm her down, tried to explain, but she threatened to call the police, she wouldn't listen to reason. He said he just wanted to see the painting, that was all he asked.

'Fuck off, you little freak,' she screamed.

That was when he lost his temper. Because she was a bully. He knew all about bullies; when he was a child, bullies who hated him and his small stature and keen mind had called him a freak, a little monster. It was the name-calling, that's what made him lose his temper. And also, his passion, his mission in life, his love for the treasures of history – that was why he'd had to make her stop, and now she was swearing at him? At him, Professor Marius Wilke? The one who had helped her find the painting in the first place?

His vengeance, his reaction to her bullying words, was not violence. No, that wasn't his way. All he wanted to do in the moment of rage was to get his book back. The one that he had signed and given to her at breakfast.

He walked to her car, jerked open the door and snatched her handbag out. The book was inside.

She screamed and swore, grabbed one of the handbag's straps and tugged. He tugged back. He was small and old and weak, she was stronger, bigger, younger, heavier. He realised it was futile.

He made a dreadful mistake, he let go of the handbag strap. Without warning.

She staggered backwards. And toppled over the bridge railing.

They heard the sickening thud as she hit something.

★   ★   ★

He was frozen in horror. He heard Bertie, dear, dear Bertie, moaning like a child. He stood there in shock, his mind racing, Bertie moaning, and then he realised he had to use his intellect to protect them both, his logic, his reasoning ability. But especially for Bertie. Bertie was like a child, he couldn't be held responsible. Bertie was the son of a neighbour when Wilke had lived in Stellenbosch. Bertie had a fall from a motorbike, years ago. There was brain damage. Bertie was living with his mother, she took care of him. But then his mother died, and Bertie had nobody, and so he took pity on Bertie and gave him a job. Be my driver, Bertie, I can't drive myself any more. That gave Bertie some sense of pride. That wasn't the act of an evil man.

He stood there in silent shock, on that bridge across the dam, and then he pulled himself together and said, 'Bertie, be quiet. It was just an accident.'

He thought through everything. He thought how it would look to others. They had been following her. Like criminals. They had forced her off the road. That looked extremely bad. Nobody was going to believe him. He had to make a plan. To protect Bertie, really just to protect Bertie.

So he made his plans.

In the dusk they found a dirt track leading down, so that they could fetch her body below the bridge, on the dry ground of the dam floor. 'It's because of the drought that she's dead, two years ago she would just have fallen in the water. The drought is to blame.'

They loaded her body into the boot of the Toyota. He sent Bertie to Grabouw to buy bleach, as much as he could find, but not more than two bottles at each shop. And bottles of water, and wash cloths, and a bucket. Wilke was well-read, he was informed, he watched all the crime programmes on TV, he knew about bleach and DNA.

He also took her cell phone out of her handbag and smashed it against the concrete of the bridge pillar, because he knew about cell phones and all they could give away.

He had waited with her until Bertie returned.

He drove ahead in her car, searching for a small farm track, and found one, the one where he'd been photographed by the leopard camera. He was so tense, so distraught, he hadn't even realised he'd been photographed.

Bertie followed. They washed her car. They stripped her, and washed her. Then they put her back in the boot. They took her handbag and clothes and car keys with them, all the empty bleach bottles, water bottles and cloths. They threw them out of the Caddy, one by one, all along the road, every five or six kilometres.

Bertie dropped him off at the house in Somerset West.

Next thing he saw the news report about the woman in the pass, and he was on the phone to Bertie asking him, Bertie, what have you done?

And Bertie said, 'She was alone in the dark, Prof. That wasn't right, you don't leave someone all alone like that in the dark.'

Bertie had gone to fetch her and arranged her up there at the lookout point.

22

On Tuesday the bank phoned Benny Griessel just before lunch.

The woman was very friendly. 'You're all over the newspapers,' she said. 'You're actually quite famous.'

He couldn't think of anything to say.

'Why didn't you tell us you were with the Hawks?'

It was right there on his application form: DPCI. But of course they had no idea that was the Hawks. Again Griessel was silent.

'We are pleased to approve your loan, Benny. May I call you Benny? Please come in and sign all the forms – and we would like to have a few photographs with you, if that's all right with you. When would suit you?'

He just shook his head. Now at last he had something that they wanted.